"I've loved this child from the beginning. But you and I are not in love with each other, Thad."

"We could be," he said, "given a little more time."

Michelle looked up at him as William curled his first around her little finger and held on tight. "What if what we feel now is as far as it gets... what if we never do fall head over heels for each other?"

"What if we don't?" Thad's voice dropped to a soft murmur. "We're sexually compatible. We both want to be married and have kids. And William needs us now."

He was beginning to make far too much sense.

"The answer is yes." She held up a palm before he could interrupt. "But there are some stipulations."

"Okay."

"We have to do a trial run."

Dear Reader,

We all want to belong. We all want a family to call our own. And most important, we all want to be loved. But what happens, I wondered, when all of that seems completely out of reach?

Thad Garner lost his mom when he was a kid and never really connected with his emotionally aloof father. Thad's an excellent E.R. doctor, but as a man looking for true love, he's not nearly as successful.

Michelle Anderson grew up with unending expectation and very little parental affection. She longed for enduring love and a happy family of her own, too. She didn't know where or when she would find it, but she was certain it wouldn't be with the sexy doc who lived across the street.

Until the morning she heard a baby's cry and saw firsthand what a natural father Thad Garner was. Thad was a lot more compassionate than she'd realized, a lot more hands-on. When he asked her if she would use her lawyerly expertise to help him figure out where and to whom the abandoned newborn baby belonged, Michelle readily agreed. Little William was darling. He deserved everything the world could give. And so, she began to realize, did Thad…

I hope you have as much fun reading this story as I did writing it.

Best wishes,

Cathy Gillen Thacker

Cathy Gillen Thacker
Found: One Baby

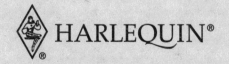

HARLEQUIN®

TORONTO • NEW YORK • LONDON
AMSTERDAM • PARIS • SYDNEY • HAMBURG
STOCKHOLM • ATHENS • TOKYO • MILAN • MADRID
PRAGUE • WARSAW • BUDAPEST • AUCKLAND

Recycling programs
for this product may
not exist in your area.

ISBN-13: 978-0-373-75258-4
ISBN-10:   0-373-75258-X

FOUND: ONE BABY

This edition published by arrangement with Harlequin Books S.A.

® and TM are trademarks of the publisher. Trademarks indicated with ® are registered in the United States Patent and Trademark Office, the Canadian Trade Marks Office and in other countries.

www.eHarlequin.com

Printed in U.S.A.

ABOUT THE AUTHOR

Cathy Gillen Thacker is married and a mother of three. She and her husband spent eighteen years in Texas, and now reside in North Carolina. Her mysteries, romantic comedies and heartwarming family stories have made numerous appearances on bestseller lists, but her best reward, she says, is knowing one of her books made someone's day a little brighter. A popular Harlequin author for many years, she loves telling passionate stories with happy endings, and thinks nothing beats a good romance and a hot cup of tea! You can visit Cathy's Web site at www.cathygillenthacker.com for more information on her upcoming and previously published books, recipes and a list of her favorite things.

Books by Cathy Gillen Thacker

This book is dedicated to sweet and patient Gwyneth May Thacker—aka the best present the Easter Bunny ever brought.

Chapter One

It wasn't the first time Michelle Anderson had noticed a "gift" left on Thad Garner's front porch. In the three months she had lived across the street from the sexy E.R. doc, a parade of hopeful single women had presented the most eligible bachelor in Summit, Texas, with everything from baked goods and homemade casseroles to gift baskets and balloons. But this was the first time she'd seen an infant car seat, diaper bag and a Moses basket left there.

Aware the latest offerings hadn't been there when she'd left the house for her early-morning run, Michelle wondered if the baby gear was supposed to be some sort of message.

If so, it was an interesting one, given that Thad Garner had the reputation of a player and the attention span of a gnat when it came to women.

The handsome thirty-three-year-old doc *said* he wanted a wife and kids. *Sooner,* rather than *later.*

But he rarely dated a woman more than two or three times before ducking out of her life as genially as he had eased in.

"The chemistry just isn't there—I'm hoping we can be friends" was what he reportedly said more often than not.

But that wasn't what the women of Summit wanted.

They wanted the passion Thad declared lacking from his side of the equation.

They also wanted, Michelle thought with a sigh, what she wanted—when the time and the man were finally right. Marriage, a fulfilling life together, kids. As well as a career. Realistically, she didn't know if it was ever going to happen for her.

Professionally and financially, everything was in place. She was thirty-two. Partner in a law practice. Had her own home. She was even considering adopting a baby on her own and—

Is that the sound of a baby crying?

It couldn't be, Michelle thought as the high-pitched sound sputtered, stopped and then resumed, now a frantic, all-out wail.

She scanned Thad's porch and yard, as well as the street. At seven on a Saturday morning, the area was usually quiet. Not today. Not with the unmistakable sound of a crying infant.

Heart pounding, Michelle jogged across the street and onto Thad's lawn. She hurried up the steps to the covered front porch of his Craftsman-style home.

Sure enough, an infant, red-faced and upset, lay in the elaborately decked-out Moses basket. He—Michelle assumed it was a boy because he was swaddled in blue—couldn't have been more than a few days old.

Heart going out to the tiny thing, Michelle knelt down on the porch. She removed the soft blanket covering the squalling child and lifted him out of the portable baby bed and into her arms.

And it was at that moment the front door jerked open.

Her too-sexy-for-his-own-good neighbor stared down at her.

And Michelle's heart took another giant leap.

THAD RUBBED HIS FACE with the palm of his hand and tried to blink himself all the way awake. "What's going on?" he demanded, sure now he had to be fantasizing. Otherwise, his gorgeous, ice princess of a neighbor would not be standing on his doorstep with a baby in her arms. "And why were you ringing the doorbell like there's a house on fire?" he asked gruffly. He'd thought he dreamed it, and had gone back to sleep—until he heard the infant crying.

Michelle Anderson's glance trailed over his bare chest and low-slung pajama pants before returning to his face. A warm flush—at odds with the cool mountain air—spread across her pretty cheeks. "I didn't ring the bell," she said.

Thad had no idea how long ago it had been when he heard the bell. Five minutes? Fifteen? It still felt like a dream. Except for the flesh-and-blood woman and tiny newborn in front of him. "You're sure standing here next to it," he observed wryly.

"Only because I wanted to ask you what was going on," she shot back.

Aware he probably should have grabbed a T-shirt before bounding outside, Thad studied Michelle and the newborn in her arms. He didn't know why, but she seemed to be accusing him of something nefarious. "You're the one with the baby," he pointed out.

Michelle patted the baby snuggled against her. The protective note in her sweetly feminine voice deepened. "True, but I'm not the one who left said baby on your front porch."

She sounded like a lawyer. "What are you talking about?"

She pointed to the infant paraphernalia next to her feet. "Someone left a baby on your doorstep."

Single women in Summit had done a lot of crazy things to get his attention, but this topped everything. "Someone should have told you it's way too late for an April Fools' joke," Thad scoffed.

"I'm well aware today is April sixth," Michelle replied coolly, "and if this *is* a ploy to get your attention, Dr. Garner, I assure you, it's not mine."

Thad looked into Michelle's face. He rubbed the last of the sleep from his eyes. "Why would anyone leave an infant with me?"

Michelle motioned at the piece of white paper wedged between the side of the baby bed and the mattress in the bottom of it. "Perhaps that envelope will tell you."

Thad knelt down to get it. His name was scrawled across the front, all right.

He tore into it and read.

Dear Thad,
Brice and Beatrix may have changed their minds about becoming parents—I haven't. It's up to your brother, Russell, to decide what to do about William, since William is his kid.

   I'm sorry it didn't work out, but again, it's not my problem. I did what I signed on to do. And that's all I'm going to do.
Sincerely,
Candace
P.S. I hope you have better luck tracking down Russell than I did.

"What the…?" Thad muttered, scanning the letter once again.

Still trying to make sense of what it said, he held it out so Michelle could read it, too. "Who are Brice and Beatrix?" she asked with a frown.

Aware the baby looked blissfully happy snuggled against his neighbor's soft breasts, Thad said, "No clue."

Michelle pulled the blanket closer around the baby's tiny body. "Candace?"

Thad shrugged and studied the wisp of dark, curling hair escaping from beneath the crocheted blue-and-white knit cap. The baby's clothes looked expensive. "Also no idea."

"But Russell…?"

"Is most definitely my brother and my only living relation," Thad replied, taking in the baby's cherubic features and fair skin. Was that his imagination or did William have the Garner nose? And Garner eyebrows? And chin?

He knew his older brother prided himself on his vagabond lifestyle, but could Russell really have turned his back on his own son? Or did he not know about him? Had the mother of this obviously unwanted child decided Russell was a bad bet as a father and put their baby up for adoption without consulting Russell? Only to have the adoptive parents back out at the last moment?

Michelle stared down at the baby as if he were the most adorable infant ever to grace the earth. Thad knew how she felt—the kid was certainly cute enough to grace a baby-food ad.

Michelle looked up at Thad. "Do you think your brother even knows he's a father?"

Thad exhaled. "Hard to say."

Irritably he scooped up the diaper bag, infant car seat and Moses basket and set them in his foyer. "Please come in," he said gruffly.

Michelle did so, albeit hesitantly, warily.

Not that she had ever been particularly friendly with him, Thad thought.

Since moving to Summit some three months earlier to take over the law practice of a retiring local barrister, she'd barely had the time of day for him. He wasn't sure why she was so aloof, at least where he was concerned. He'd never been anything but cordial to the attractive attorney.

Of course they hadn't encountered each other all that often. She worked from nine to six Monday through Friday. His shifts were generally twelve hours and varied according to the demands of the Summit, Texas, emergency room.

Nevertheless, he'd had a hard time keeping his eyes off the willowy strawberry blonde.

Michelle Anderson carried herself with the self-confident grace of an accomplished career woman. On workdays she could usually be seen in sophisticated business suits and heels. On weekends and evenings, she was much more casual.

This morning, she was wearing a pair of navy running shorts that made the most of her long, shapely legs, a hot-pink-and-navy T-shirt that paid similar homage to her breasts. Her running shoes and socks were white. Her hair was caught up in a ponytail on the back of her head, and the few escaped tendrils were attractively mussed. Her peaches-and-cream complexion had a healthy glow, while her emerald-green eyes held the skepticism of a woman who had seen and heard way too much in the course of her profession.

But then, Thad thought, walking over to snag a navy-blue T-shirt off the back of the sofa and pull it on, so had he…

"Well?" Michelle asked, bouncing slightly to comfort the now squirming newborn, as Thad slid on a pair of moccasins and came back to stand beside her. "Does that letter make any sense at all to you?" she demanded.

Thad watched the baby root around as if looking for a nipple. "Unfortunately, yes," he admitted reluctantly, not proud of this part of his family heritage. Spying a baby bottle in the pocket of the infant seat, he plucked it out and unscrewed the lid.

The formula smelled fresh. He screwed the top back on and handed it to her. "My brother is as reckless and shortsighted as they come."

"Meaning?" Michelle offered the bottle to William and smiled when he latched on immediately.

Thad frowned. "It's possible Russell's gotten himself in a mess and left me to clean up." And that was all Thad was prepared to say until he had talked to his only sibling.

At Thad's invitation, Michelle sat down on the sofa and gave William his bottle while Thad went off to make some phone calls.

When he returned some thirty minutes later, he was dressed as if for work, his broad shoulders and impossibly masculine chest covered by a starched green shirt and tie, his trim waist, hips and long, sinewy legs draped in khaki dress slacks. His custom-made leather boots were buffed to a soft sheen.

He smelled…so good. Like the forest after a drenching spring rain. And he looked great, too—his square jaw newly shaven, his golden-brown eyes alert with interest. "I left messages for Russell everywhere," he reported grimly.

Trying not to notice how the early-morning sunlight streaming in through the windows glimmered in his short, sandy-brown hair, Michelle shifted William to her shoulder to burp him. Up close, she couldn't help but notice—once again—how ruggedly handsome Thad was. No wonder all the women in town were wild about him. When she tore her gaze from his chiseled jaw and sensual lips, it was only to meet the warm intimacy of his amber eyes.

Finally she found her voice. "Any idea how long it will take for your brother to get back to you?" she asked, surprised at how casual and unaffected she sounded.

Thad looked unhappy. "No telling." He clipped a pager and cell phone to his belt, searched around for his keys. "Russell could be in any time zone. He's a photojournalist for a wire news service, always off on assignment somewhere, but he checks his messages every day, unless he's in a war zone. Then, of course, it can be harder to get in touch with him."

Michelle was rubbing William's back gently. "What are you going to do?"

Thad eyed her reluctantly. "That's what I wanted to talk to you about." He sat down next to her and smiled tenderly at the baby, who was looking back at him with sleepy blue eyes. "I'm due at the E.R. in twenty minutes. I'm trying to get someone to cover my shift for me. Meanwhile, I need someone to watch William." He offered his index finger to the baby and grinned when William instinctively wrapped his tiny fist around it and held on tight.

Anxiously, Thad looked back at Michelle. "You know any babysitters I could call on short notice?"

Michelle knew what he was really asking. "You can't take him with you to the hospital?"

Thad shook his head. "It'd be a bad idea. Too many germs in the E.R."

He had a point there. She looked down at her tiny charge. It didn't matter what she thought of Thad. This child needed tender loving care. "How old do you think he is?" she asked softly, smiling when William finally let out a healthy-sounding burp.

Thad chuckled, too. "A few days. Maybe."

And already abandoned. Michelle felt tears welling in her eyes. "That's what I thought, too," she murmured thickly. She wished she could simply take William to her place and give him the home he deserved. But life was never that simple.

Wishes were never granted that easily. She would not get the baby she wanted in her life this way.

"So back to the babysitter dilemma," Thad persisted, oblivious to the yearning nature of her thoughts. "Any idea who I could call?"

"Besides any of your legion of female admirers?" she quipped, offering the last of the bottle to William.

"I'm serious."

So was she. Michelle tested the waters with an idea. "Violet Hunter knows a lot about kids."

"We dated a couple times, when I first came to town."

So Michelle had heard. The pretty single mom had been one of Thad's most persistent admirers.

"It was about six months after her husband died," Thad continued cryptically. "It didn't work out. From what I can tell, although it's been about two years now, she's still pretty vulnerable."

Michelle had met the twenty-nine-year-old nurse—and her two little girls—at a charity fund-raiser the previous summer. She was very nice. And very much in the market for another husband.

She looked at him, waiting.

"I don't want to give Violet the wrong idea," Thad said finally.

Michelle studied him. Close up, he didn't appear to be the kind of guy who enjoyed stringing women along. In fact, the opposite. Life had taught her that appearances could be deceptive. She did better relying on facts in her personal life, just as she did in her practice of the law.

"And the wrong idea would be?" she probed.

Thad regarded her with the patient cool of an expert witness. "That something might be possible when it's not." Regret turned down the corners of his mouth. "And if I call

Violet—or someone else I've dated—and tell them I need help with the baby I suddenly have on my hands…"

"You'd probably be getting more than chicken enchilada casserole on your front porch," Michelle said wryly.

"Exactly."

"Whereas if you were to put me in charge…"

He suddenly seemed defensive. "It's pretty clear where you stand regarding dating me."

"But you've never asked me out, so I've never had the opportunity to turn you down."

"But you would," Thad countered.

True. If only because she didn't want to end up wasting her time again on something that was never going to happen. Only this time, given Thad's rep with the local ladies, she would know that going in. Deciding, since they were neighbors, it was best simply to be honest, she shrugged. "I don't date players."

His lips tightened. "I'm not a player."

Michelle kept her eyes off the sinewy lines of his shoulders and chest. She did not need to remember how he looked clad only in a low-slung cotton pajama bottom, or be thinking about the crisp, dark hair arrowing straight down the goody line. She closed her mind to any further licentious thoughts. "Right."

"I'm just honest about whether or not I see a future with a woman."

Doing her best to slow her racing pulse, she got a hold of her out-of-control fantasies and retorted, "And you usually don't."

"Usually isn't always," he replied cryptically.

Which meant what? Michelle wondered. He'd had his heart broken, too?

Disconcerted—because that would give them something

in common—she returned her gaze to the newborn nestled in her arms.

If William were *her* baby…

But he wasn't, Michelle reminded herself firmly.

Still, the little guy was here now. He needed someone to watch over him until this mess could be sorted out. Someone who wouldn't leave him on Thad Garner's doorstep all by himself.

"Believe me," Thad said, sounding as protective toward this tiny baby as she was, "if I had any other job, I'd stay and take care of the little fella myself. But I can't leave the E.R. short-staffed. We've got the only trauma center in the entire county."

Lives depended on Thad.

Just as William, it seemed, was momentarily depending on her.

Before Michelle could stop herself, she was pushing aside every self-protective instinct she had and volunteering. "Fine. I'll do it."

Thad's eyebrows lifted in amazement. "You sure?" he said finally, standing. "It's going to be twelve hours, unless I'm able to find someone to cover the rest of my shift for me."

Forcing herself to shove aside the memory of another child, another time, Michelle stood, too. There would be no such heartbreak this time because she wouldn't allow herself to get that involved with William or Thad.

Loving the way the now sleeping William snuggled against her, she brushed off Thad's concern. "I didn't have much planned for today, anyway," she fibbed. Her flower beds could wait.

Thad breathed a sigh of relief. "Thanks. I really appreciate it."

Michelle had a few stipulations of her own. "I want to watch him at my house, though." The less she knew about Thad, the less time spent in his abode, the better.

"Of course." Thad gently brushed his fingertips across William's velvety cheek.

The air between the three of them reverberated with tenderness.

With apparent effort, Thad dropped his hand, stepped back and looked over at the baby gear in the foyer. "I hope everything you're going to need is here."

Michelle lowered her face to William and smelled…spit-up. Knowing that was something that could easily be taken care of, she said quietly, "If you'll carry the stuff across the street, I'll sort through it."

"No problem." He plucked up the items and followed her out the front door. "I owe you big-time for this," he told her solemnly, falling into step beside her.

"Yes," Michelle agreed. "You do."

WHERE TO START? Michelle wondered as soon as the door shut behind Thad, and she and William were alone. She supposed it best to change William's diaper.

She slung the diaper bag over her shoulder and carried him upstairs to her bedroom. His eyes were open again as she laid him gently down on the soft cotton quilt on her bed. "You know, we hear about things like this all the time," she told him as she pulled a diaper and a packet of wipes from the bag. "Babies being left in the strangest places. I just want you to know that you shouldn't take it personally. Candace was only doing what she thought best, taking you to your uncle Thad's house."

Although why Candace had simply left him in the Moses basket on the front porch was anyone's guess. "But I don't want you to worry," Michelle continued reassuringly. "Because we are going to find your parents and get this all straightened out."

One way or another, they would find a great home for William. Even if it meant calling the police and social services.

"In the meantime, I'm going to take care of you today, and then your uncle Thad is going to look after you. And before you know it, this little blip in your existence will be over. And it'll all be good."

All she had to do, Michelle thought as she went about getting everything she needed out of the diaper bag, was not get emotionally involved in a situation that was ultimately a win-lose proposition for her.

Winning, because she got to spend time with the most adorable baby she had ever seen.

And losing, because she was going to have to let him go.

Just as she'd had to let Jared and his son, Jimmy, go.

And that was as painful an event as ever, Michelle mused, unsnapping the legs of William's designer duds.

Before she could get the diaper off, her phone rang.

Seeing Thad Garner's name flash on the caller-ID screen, she grabbed the portable off the bedside table.

"How are things going?" he asked.

It was ridiculous how glad she was to hear his voice. She hit the speaker button on the receiver and set it on the bed. Doing her best to play it cool, she said, "You just left him five minutes ago!"

"More like seven." Thad paused. "It sounds quiet."

Talk about overprotective! "He seems happy enough," Michelle allowed.

"He's awake?"

"Yes. I'm in the process of changing his diaper."

"While we talk?"

"Believe it or not, I can multitask." She used a baby wipe on William.

"How does the diaper area look? Everything okay?"

William turned his head slightly toward the sound of Thad's voice.

Michelle smiled. "As far as I can tell. It looks like he had a circumcision."

"Did they leave any antibiotic ointment for the stitches?"

"Yes." Figuring he would know, she asked, "How often are you supposed to apply it?"

"A very thin layer three times a day."

Michelle made a note of that. "Since we don't know when it was done last, should I go ahead and do that now? Or wait till later?"

"Go ahead and put some on now just to be on the safe side."

Michelle did as directed.

Thad paused. "Is there a pharmacy label on the ointment?"

Once again, they were of one mind. Had there been a label, there would have been a patient last name and a prescribing physician and hospital or pharmacy name, as well. "No. It may have been on the box the ointment came in—but that's not with his belongings." She confirmed this with a second look through the bag.

"Too bad. It would have helped to have more to go on than first names."

Michelle agreed wholeheartedly. Right now, of the four people ostensibly involved in this fiasco, they only knew how to contact one, and he might be out of the country! "Did you hear from your brother?" she asked, hoping that might have been the real reason for the call.

"Not yet." Thad sighed his frustration.

As long as she had "the doctor" on the line, Michelle asked, "Would it be okay if I gave William a sponge bath? He smells a little like spit-up."

"How's his umbilical cord?"

She checked it out. "Kind of, um, brown. Still hanging on."

"Not infected?"

"No."

"I think a sponge bath would be okay," Thad said in that thoughtful voice doctors used when tending to patients. "Just make sure the water temperature is lukewarm. And don't get the cord wet—keep that area dry."

Michelle resnapped the onesie and tucked the blanket in around William to keep him warm. "I'll go to Dr. Greene's Web site on the Internet and read up on the proper procedure before I start, just to make sure I do everything correctly."

Another pause. "You know about that?"

Michelle tried not to take offense at the surprise in Thad's voice. "All my friends back in Dallas have babies. All of them use that Web site as their primary reference."

"No wonder you seem so at ease with a newborn," he said.

That wasn't why.

But Michelle didn't want to tell him about the year she had spent taking care of another infant, only to lose him—and his father—in the end.

"Anything else you need?" Thad asked helpfully.

Michelle studied the contents of the diaper bag. "As far as I can tell, there appear to be enough diapers, clothing and formula to last a couple of days." She wondered if Thad would even *have* the baby that long. She knew better than anyone that the situation could change in an instant, that Brice and Beatrix or Candace or even Russell could show up to claim the baby. Which again was why she needed not to become too attached or overly involved in this situation.

Oblivious to her concerns, Thad continued, "If you need anything else, let me know. I'll pick it up on the way back."

This was suddenly getting way too cozy for comfort.

Reminded of the last time she'd had her heart broken, Michelle picked up William and held him. "Aren't you supposed to be at work?" Michelle asked impatiently, beginning to see why women fell so hard for the notoriously sexy doctor.

"In two minutes." Thad paused. "I just wanted to check with you before I actually went into the hospital and let you know how to page me in case anything else comes up." Thad gave her the number. "Call me if you need me. Otherwise, I'll check in with you later," he promised before he hung up.

With a sigh, Michelle turned back to the fragile bundle in her arms. "Looks like it's just you and me, little guy," she said. She smiled, realizing he was already fast asleep. "At least until your uncle Thad returns."

Chapter Two

Thad expected to have half-a-dozen calls from Michelle Anderson during the day.

There were no phone calls.

And the two times he did call her, just to check in, she had sounded a little exasperated.

He guessed he couldn't blame her.

She probably thought he didn't trust her to take care of William in his absence. Nothing could have been further from the truth. Like animals, children knew instinctively whom they could trust and draw comfort from. William had recognized Michelle for the maternal soul she was from the moment she picked him up and cradled him gently in her arms.

Still, the moment his shift was up, Thad headed out the door and drove the short distance home. He parked in his driveway, then headed across the street.

As he approached the front porch of her Arts and Crafts–style home, he noticed the windows were open. Mounting the front steps, he heard Michelle singing softly. He glanced through the window. She was sitting in an old-fashioned rocking chair he hadn't seen earlier, William in her arms.

Thad couldn't tell if the baby was awake or asleep—he

couldn't see William's face—but the moment was so tender and loving it stopped him in his tracks. This, he thought, was what parenthood should be about. This was the kind of life he and his brother should have had as kids, even after their mother died.

But they hadn't. And there was no going back. Only forward. To the family he wanted to create.

All he needed was a woman to love.

He rapped on the screen.

The lovely vocal rendition of "Brahms' Lullaby" stopped. Michelle rose slowly and walked over to open the door and let him in. She had changed into vintage jeans and a pale blue knit shirt that clung to her curves. Her apparently just-shampooed hair had dried in a tangle of soft, strawberry-blond curls. He had never seen her wear it that way, but he liked it as much as the sleek, straight style she usually wore.

"William looks…happy," Thad noted. And so did she.

A pretty pink blush lit Michelle's cheeks. "He's very happy," she said, meeting Thad's eyes, "as long as he's being held." She frowned in concern. "Every time I get him to sleep and put him down, he wakes up after about ten minutes and completely freaks out."

"Probably remembering…"

"Waking up alone on your front porch?" Michelle asked. "That's what I was thinking."

Thad shook his head. His brother was very much like their father had been while he was alive. Neither held much regard for familial responsibility or blood ties. Their lives were all about the latest career challenge.

Thad shoved his hands through his hair in frustration. "Damn Russell," he muttered.

Michelle exhaled softly. "Haven't heard from him, I take it?"

"No. And I've left several messages." Thad felt the vibration of his phone. He took it off his belt clip, looked at the caller ID. Speak of the devil. "Finally!" Scowling, Thad put the phone to his ear. "Where are you?" he barked.

"I'm on assignment in Thailand. What's the emergency?" Russell demanded, sounding equally irritated.

"A baby was left on my porch this morning." Briefly, Thad explained.

Russell swore like a sailor who'd just found out his shore leave was canceled. But typically, he offered no explanation or apology.

Thad pressed on. "Did you know you were having a baby with Candace when you left the country?"

"I assumed she was pregnant," Russell retorted, surprisingly matter-of-fact. "I didn't know for sure."

And obviously hadn't bothered to find out, Thad thought irritably. "Why didn't you mention it to me?" he demanded.

"Because her pregnancy wasn't relevant to my life," Russell grumbled.

Figuring he was going to need legal advice sooner rather than later, Thad activated the speaker on his phone and motioned Michelle closer, so she could listen in on the conversation.

"What do you mean Candace's pregnancy wasn't relevant to your life?" Thad asked.

Russell exhaled. "It was a surrogate arrangement. I donated sperm for a couple of friends."

Okay. That made slightly more sense. Thad withdrew the pen and notepad he habitually carried in his shirt pocket. He wrote "Help me out here" on a slip of paper and handed it to Michelle.

She edged closer, concern on her face. "According to the

note left with baby William, Brice and Beatrix changed their minds about becoming parents," Thad told his brother.

"You'll have to ask Candace Wright about that," Russell insisted.

Thad jotted down the last name of William's birth mother. "Do you have a phone number?"

Another disgruntled sigh. "She lives in Big Spring. That's all I know."

"What about Brice and Beatrix, the adoptive couple?"

"The Johnsons live in San Angelo. Listen, I can't do anything from here—you're going to have to straighten it all out."

"How?" Thad shot back, aggrieved his brother could be so cold. "I don't have paternity."

"Neither do I. I signed away all my rights at the fertility clinic before the surrogate was even impregnated."

"We're going to need a copy of those papers ASAP," Michelle told Thad, switching into lawyer mode.

"Who is that?" Russell demanded.

"Michelle Anderson," she introduced herself. "I'm a neighbor of your brother's—I found the baby."

"She's also an attorney," Thad interjected.

Michelle asked Russell, "Is there any way we can look at those papers you signed?"

Russell harrumphed. "They're in one of the boxes I left in Thad's attic. If you can find them, you can have 'em. Aside from that, I don't want anything to do with this. Like Candace Wright, I've done my part."

It wasn't that simple, Thad knew. "If what Candace said is true…if Brice and Beatrix have changed their minds about taking William into their family… Genetically, the child is half yours."

"Not to my way of thinking," Russell snapped.

"He's a Garner." And that, Thad thought, should mean something.

Russell scoffed. "What would I do with a kid? I don't have a home and I don't want one."

Every fiber of Thad's being told him it would be a mistake just to walk away. Anger rising, he said, "You can't just stand by and do nothing while this child you had a hand in creating is abandoned."

"Sure I can," Russell replied. "And you know why? Because it would be best. The kid doesn't need a father like the one we had. And that's what I am. However, if you think you can do better, if you want to jump in, Thad, be my guest. Just leave me out of it."

The connection ended with a decisive click.

Thad locked gazes with Michelle, not sure whether he was sorry or glad she had heard all that. He swore. "What a mess."

YES, MICHELLE THOUGHT. It was one heck of a mess.

Deciding it was time to try again, she carried the sleeping William over to the elaborately lined Moses basket, and set him down gently on his back. She tucked a blanket around him to keep him warm. Relieved he still appeared to be asleep, at least for the moment, she walked over to the window where Thad was standing. "I'm not sure I should be involved in this situation."

Thad looked surprised, then confused. "You're a lawyer."

Her pulse picked up as she pointed out, "I'm not *your* lawyer."

Thad tilted his head. "You could be."

She kept her expression impassive. "This is a family-law case."

He raised an eyebrow. "And you have a background in family law. A pretty good one, from what I've heard."

That was then, Michelle thought. This was now. And she knew better these days. She lifted her hands in a vague gesture of dissatisfaction and stepped away. "I did so much of it the first five years out of law school that I burned out on it. My current practice focuses on the needs of small business, wills and estate planning, real estate and consumer law. My law partner—Glenn York—does all the divorce, custody and adoption cases for our firm."

"I know his reputation. He's very good." Thad paused. He glanced over at the sleeping William, then back to Michelle. "I'd still prefer you handle it."

His was not an uncommon reaction. People with legal trouble often latched on to the first person who appeared able to help them out of it, without bothering to verify credentials or search out expertise in that specific area of the law. "You don't even know me," she said.

"You've handled the situation well so far."

That wasn't the only reason, Michelle decided. "You're embarrassed by your brother's attitude, aren't you?"

A muscle worked in Thad's jaw. "Wouldn't you be?"

Michelle tried not to think how easy it was to be here with Thad like this. She shrugged. "I learned a long time ago not to judge people by the messes they get themselves into." She had always been trained to look at both sides of every issue. "Besides, it sounds as if your brother was trying to do a good deed for someone. It just didn't turn out the way he expected."

Thad sobered. "I hadn't thought about it that way."

Michelle called upon even more of her law-school training. "Your brother may change his mind about the child."

Thad's mouth took on a downward slant. "No. He won't."

"How can you be so sure?"

"Because of the way we grew up." Thad's mood turned reflective. "Our mom was really great—loving and fun, smart and kind—but she died from an aneurysm when Russell and I were in elementary school. We barely knew our dad—he was a geologist for an oil company. I've no doubt he loved us in his way, but he wasn't interested in being a hands-on parent. Nevertheless, he left the project he was working on in South America and came back to Summit to take care of us." He exhaled. "For the next ten years or so, he worked assignments around the state. When we hit our teens and were old enough to stay alone, he went back to the more exciting gigs in South and Central America. From that point on, until he died five years ago, we rarely saw him because he was just never home."

Michelle touched Thad's arm gently. "That sounds lonely."

Thad glanced at her hand, then said, "Summit's a close-knit community. We had a lot of people looking out for us. Plenty to eat. And the house across the street to live in."

But, Michelle speculated, not what he had obviously wanted most—a loving, emotionally engaged and interested parent on the premises.

"What was your childhood like?" Thad asked, his rumbling drawl sending shivers over her skin.

She figured she might as well be honest, too. "I grew up in a well-to-do suburban enclave of Dallas. I was an only child of two very loving but ambitious people." She paused. "So let's just say, for me, failure in any venue was not an option."

Thad chuckled sympathetically. "You're giving me new appreciation for my laissez-faire teens."

Michelle sighed. The understanding look on his face soon had her confiding further in him. "Don't get me wrong. I had plenty of attention and everything I needed to succeed. Including special tutors and private coaches when necessary."

Thad seemed to know instinctively there was more. "But...?"

"There were times when I felt as if I had been born on a treadmill set at high speed with no way to get off." Times when she had felt she would never please her folks no matter how much she accomplished. Michelle forced herself to go on. "My parents were both tenured university professors and department chairs. When they weren't hovering over me, urging me to greater heights, they worked all the time."

William stirred and began to whimper again. She went over to pick him up before he began to wail in earnest. Soothing him with a cuddle and a kiss, Michelle walked back to Thad.

"That sounds rough," he said.

Michelle nodded and handed the baby to him. "Too much so for my folks," she admitted, watching with pleasure as William snuggled up to Thad every bit as easily as he had snuggled up to her. Then she frowned. "My mom and dad both died of stress-related illnesses a few years ago. Their health problems spurred me to reevaluate my own life. I decided I didn't want to continue to live in the big city, so I began saving money and looking around for a place to live a quieter life."

"I know what you mean. I went to medical school and did my E.R. residency in Houston. By the time I'd finished, I'd had enough of rush-hour traffic and crowds. When there was an opening at the Summit hospital, I jumped at it."

William's lashes shut. His breathing grew deep and even once again.

"But we digress," Michelle said.

Thad cast a loving glance at the infant in his arms. "Yes," he said softly. "We do."

Forcing herself to pull back emotionally, before she got in

way over her head, Michelle said, "You need to get this situation with William sorted out as soon as possible."

Before either of them fell even more in love with this abandoned little boy.

THE FIRST ORDER of business, they both decided, after they had resettled the sleeping William in his bed, was to get the addresses and phone numbers of the people involved. That turned out to be easy enough. An Internet search quickly gave them contact information for Candace Wright, as well as Brice and Beatrix Johnson.

Aware he was so far out of his depth it wasn't funny, Thad asked, "Any advice on how I should handle this?"

Michelle glanced sideways at him, reminding him, "I'm not going to represent you."

Thad wondered if she had any idea how beautiful she looked in the soft light of her elegantly decorated living room, feet propped up on the coffee table, laptop computer settled on her jean-clad thighs. He propped up his feet on the coffee table, too, next to hers. "You could still advise me as a friend."

Her eyes remained on the screen as she studied the information there. She typed in the print command. "Are we friends?"

Somewhere in the too-quiet depths of her house, he heard a laser printer start up. "I think we're getting there." As she put her laptop aside and moved to stand, he inhaled the orange-blossom fragrance of her shampoo.

He stood, too. "Why? Does that bother you?"

He followed her down the hall to the kitchen. A home-office space had been built into one wall, with floor-to-ceiling kitchen cabinets on either side. The printer was on the shelf above the desk. She plucked several pages out of the tray and gave him a look of lawyerly calm. "These are highly unusual circumstances."

No argument there. Thad shrugged, aware he hadn't been this affected by a woman in a long time. If ever. "What better way to get to know each other?"

Her lips curved cynically. "I hope you're not hitting on me."

Was he? "Wouldn't think of it." Thad matched her semi-amused tone.

Silence fell between them. Knowing this would all go a lot easier if Michelle were there to help him and their tiny charge, Thad walked back to the living room with her. "Just help me get through the rest of the weekend," he proposed.

In his bed, William pushed out his lower lip in indignation and began to whimper once again.

"Then if I need to hire someone, I'll do it on Monday morning." He picked up William and cradled him in his arms. The little guy couldn't have weighed more than eight pounds and still had the faint redness of skin all newborns had. Yet he already had so much personality. "I don't want to screw this up. This little guy has already been through enough." Thad fought the unexpected tightness in his throat, continued in a voice that sounded rusty, even to him. "And since my brother is not acting responsibly…"

Michelle turned away, but not before Thad thought he saw a glint of empathetic tears in her green eyes. She cleared her throat. "Speaking of Russell, maybe you should try to find whatever it is he signed and make sure those papers state what he thinks they do."

"Good point." Legal jargon could be as confusing as medical terminology. "You want to come over with us, help me search?"

Surprise mingled briefly with disappointment in her eyes. "You're taking the baby tonight, then?"

"I figured I'd keep William at my place tonight since you had him all day." Thad gazed at Michelle. She looked like she'd just lost her best friend. "You can stay over, too." The invitation was out before he could think.

She took it completely the wrong way. The droll expression was back on her face. "Uh, thanks, but…no."

He held up one palm. "I'll be the perfect gentleman."

She rolled her eyes. "I'm sure you would be."

She fit the crocheted cap on William's head and helped Thad bundle him up in a blanket. When that was done, she picked up the diaper bag and Moses basket, while he held the door for both of them.

Together, they strolled down the front walk and across the street. Thad led the way up his front porch, wishing he'd thought to turn on the lights before he'd gone over to Michelle's home.

"So, my rep is that bad?" Thad shifted William to one arm while he unlocked the door and hit the lights.

"Or good." Michelle preceded Thad inside in another drift of orange blossom. For the first time he realized how disorderly his home was.

"Excuse me?" he asked in confusion.

"It all depends on how you look at it," she explained.

Thad switched on more lamps, wishing he'd thought to vacuum or dust in the past month, instead of sitting around reading medical journals and working out at the hospital fitness center in his spare time.

"Please continue," he prodded her.

She looked him straight in the eye. "You've got a reputation for dating around, not sleeping around."

"Good to know," he said.

The sparkle was back in her eyes. "Isn't it?"

Thad figured it wouldn't hurt to flirt. Especially since she'd started it. "As long as we're on the subject, want to know what your rep in the community is?"

DID SHE WANT to know?

His goading look was all the provocation she needed. "Well, I guess now I have to know."

Thad put William over his shoulder and gently patted his back, then turned his attention back to her. "Ice princess."

Okay, that hurt. A little. Especially since she'd done nothing to deserve it.

She made her eyes go wide. "Really?"

"Mm-hm." Thad stepped closer, still patting William on the back. "Word is, you've been asked out by at least twenty guys—"

"I think that's a small exaggeration," she said.

"—and said no to every single one," Thad finished smugly, leaving no doubt that he'd been investigating the details of her romantic life, or lack thereof, too.

She shrugged, aware her pulse was racing, and defended herself. "Well, that's because I won't go out with someone if I don't see hope of anything…happening."

A smile tugging at the corners of his mouth, he leaned down so they were practically nose to nose. "How can you know if you don't go out with them?"

"I just do."

He let his gaze drift over her slowly, before returning to her eyes. "See, I don't buy that," he told her with lazy male confidence. "I don't think you can begin to know someone unless you spend one-on-one time together. You've got to take a risk—"

Michelle smirked. "Well, I hear you've done plenty of that."

"—to reap rewards." He sneaked a peek at the baby on his shoulder. He grinned when he realized that William was sound asleep again. He walked over to the Moses basket and gently laid the baby down, covering him with a blanket.

Trying not to notice how naturally Thad had taken to being a daddy figure to the abandoned little boy, Michelle rocked forward on her toes.

The thought of Thad reaping rewards with any other woman bothered her more than it should. Marshaling all her defenses, she asked sweetly, "How's that method working out for you so far?"

"I haven't hit pay dirt yet." His gaze slid past the delicate hollow of her throat, to her lips and then her eyes. "I will."

She took a deep breath, dropped her gaze. Then found herself remembering the way he'd looked, shirtless and just out of bed, that morning. Flushing, she tore her eyes from the masculine contours of his chest. "*Sure* you will."

"Make fun all you like," he said. He stepped closer. "You need to take more risks."

His words hit a chord. She'd heard the same from others, too. "Just see if you can find the papers," she instructed irritably, deciding Dr. Thad Garner was the last man she would ever get involved with.

Thad sighed. "Wish me luck. That attic is a mess."

"IT'S NOT THERE," Thad reported in frustration a short time later.

He'd only been up in the attic twenty minutes, Michelle thought. She removed the bottle she'd been heating from the bowl of warm water. "Are you sure?"

Thad looked at William, who was lying patiently in his

Moses basket, eyes wide open, trying awkwardly to get his thumb to his mouth. "I checked through the most recent boxes."

Which meant Thad hadn't checked through everything belonging to his brother, Michelle deduced. "Maybe it's in an older box," she suggested, wiping the outside of the bottle dry. "Do you want me to go up and look?"

Thad glanced at her clothes. "It's kind of grimy up there," he warned.

Michelle tested the bottle on the inside of her wrist. "Not a problem. You'll have to feed William, though."

"He's ready to eat again?"

"Yes, he is." Michelle handed Thad the bottle of formula. Thad smiled, as if he relished his first chance to give William a bottle.

"You know, we could probably just wait and ask Candace Wright."

"That's assuming we can find her and she'll talk to us. She may not. In any case, it's best to be as prepared as you can be before you walk into a situation like this." She sighed. "So if Russell thinks the papers he signed are in the attic, I think we need to do everything possible to find them. Because if we can find them, then we will know what attorney he used to prepare them."

"What if they didn't use an attorney? What if they just went online and printed out some do-it-yourself forms and signed those?"

Michelle exhaled. "Then none of what they've done may be legal. But again, we're getting ahead of ourselves." She held up a staying hand. "How do I get to the attic?"

Thad picked up William and the bottle. "We'll walk you up there."

Thad motioned her up the stairs. Past the master bedroom, with its heavy mahogany furniture and big, comfortable-looking bed. There was a stack of books and what looked like medical journals on both nightstands. Baskets of what looked like clean, unfolded laundry, and an overflowing hamper. On down the hall, past another bath and bedroom, decorated in teenage-boy motif, with a big sign on the door that read: Russell's Room—No One Else Allowed. Next to that was a study, with a desk and cozy leather armchair and ottoman. Along one wall was a stack of gift boxes, reminding Michelle of all the women in town who were chasing him. Before she could stop herself, she blurted, "What's this? The trophy room?"

"I'm planning to donate it all. I just can't do it anywhere in town. 'Cause someone will know and then I'll hurt somebody's feelings...and I don't want to do that."

She could see he was serious. "It must be hard to be you," she said dryly.

He returned her droll look and opened a door leading to the third floor. "Up there."

Michelle hit the switch next to the door. Light flooded the third floor and spilled down the rough wooden stairs. "Thanks."

Thad wandered back in the direction they'd come. "William, let's go into the master bedroom and have ourselves a bottle, shall we?"

Shaking her head, Michelle headed up the stairs. Thad was right. It was a mess. And a pretty big one. Most of it seemed to be Russell's, judging by the name scrawled in black Magic Marker on the sides of boxes.

She began looking. And looking. And looking. Finally, thirty minutes later, she hit the jackpot. Or at least she hoped she had. She found a metal lockbox, the kind where people tended to store their important papers. Only problem was, she noted, it was locked.

Footsteps sounded on the stairs. Thad came up to stand beside her. "Any luck?"

She waved her find. "This could be it."

Thad towered over her, six feet two inches of attractive single male. "I didn't know he had that up here," he murmured in a low, sexy voice.

Once again, Michelle forced herself to set her attraction to the handsome doctor aside. She moved past him and headed briskly down the stairs. "Where's William?"

Thad followed laconically. "In his Moses basket, asleep."

Which meant she now had Thad's undivided attention, at least for the next ten minutes or so, until William awakened again. She ignored the tingling in her midriff and forced herself to stay focused on the task. "You don't happen to have a key for this?"

He shook his head.

"How about a paper clip?"

"In my study."

They peeked in the master bedroom, where William was sleeping, then ducked into the study, opened a desk drawer and rummaged around. Finally he produced a paper clip and handed it over.

She could feel him watching her as she sat on the edge of the desk and began to work on the lock.

She looked up. The intent, appreciative, all-male look in his eyes made her catch her breath. "What are you thinking?" she demanded.

Thad tucked a finger beneath her chin, moved in closer. "This."

Chapter Three

Michelle had plenty of time to duck her head and step away—if she wanted to avoid the kiss.

She didn't.

Maybe because kissing him was all she'd been thinking about since he'd answered the door that morning, fresh out of bed.

Actually, she reminded herself sagely, the zing of awareness had happened a lot sooner than that. He'd caught her attention as soon as she realized who was living across the street from her.

The parade of women making their way to his front door—plus his reputation as a love-'em-and-leave-'em type—had kept her from acting on that purely physical attraction.

But coming face-to-face with him this morning, being close enough to touch that powerful, masculine body, had forced her to see him in a new light.

Not just as a neighbor or a guy she was too wary of to befriend.

But as a man who conjured up the kind of romantic daydreams and pure, physical lust she didn't know she possessed. And seeing him with William, knowing how deeply he cared about family, even when it seemed that the only family he had left didn't care all that much about him, had added another dimension to the mystery that was Thad.

So when Thad angled his head and his face drifted slowly, inevitably closer to hers, Michelle gave in to the curiosity that had plagued her for months now and let it happen.

She opened her mouth slightly and let his warm, sensual lips make contact with hers. And then suddenly his arms were around her, dragging her closer, so that every inch of her was pressed against every inch of him. Hardness to softness, heat pressed to heat, she was wrapped in a cage of hard male muscle and passionate determination. Her heart beat wildly and she tilted her head back in open surrender. His tongue swept into her mouth, blazing a path that was as tender as it was fiery. She stroked her tongue against the potent pressure of his, knowing she hadn't made out like this…since… Had she *ever* made out like this? Had her insides ever sizzled from just a kiss?

Michelle didn't think so. Which was why, she realized abruptly, she couldn't let it continue. She'd be in *way* over her head.

She flattened her hands on the hard wall of his chest and tore her lips from his. "Stop!"

Just that swiftly, Thad did.

He drew back, loosening his hold on her, not letting go completely. "What's wrong?"

She lifted her brow. "You even have to ask?"

This time, he did release her.

He stepped back and settled on the edge of his desk. Long legs stretched out in front of him, hands braced casually on either side of him, he met her gaze. "I have to admit…I'm confused," he murmured, making no effort to hide his continuing desire, "since I thought we were getting along like a house on fire."

They had been. She hitched in a breath and qualified, "For all the wrong reasons."

His brow furrowed.

She held up her hands in a gesture that warded off further intimacy. "It's not you and me, Thad. It's the *situation*. Our emotions are heightened. Finding William this morning… well, it upset our whole world. So naturally we have a lot of extra adrenaline and emotional energy to burn off, and we did that by ending up in each other's arms."

The look he gave her was skeptical. One corner of his just-kissed mouth quirked up, reminding her of how great he tasted. "That all sounds very reasonable—except for one thing. I work in a hospital trauma center, Michelle. I'm used to a hell of a lot more upset and stress."

She flushed with an embarrassment she could not contain. Held his eyes with effort. "So maybe I'm the only one with an excess of adrenaline and emotion."

He sobered immediately. "Well, maybe—but we still haven't figured out how we're going to handle this situation with William."

Trying hard not to focus on the *we* in his approach, Michelle decided more physical distance between them was needed. She sat down on the leather reading chair in the corner and went back to working on the lock. "First of all, William was left in your care, so it's really your call how you want to proceed."

He settled more comfortably on the edge of his desk. "I want your professional advice."

Michelle slipped into the much more comfortable lawyer mode. "I suggest you speak to Candace Wright first—since she is the person who apparently left William in your care, and Beatrix and Brice Johnson next. Find out what went wrong with the surrogate arrangement and if the Johnsons really have changed their mind, or if this is all some sort of big misunderstanding."

Thad paused, looking none too happy about the possibility someone might want William back. "You think it's possible the surrogate and the Johnsons somehow got their signals crossed?"

Michelle had stepped into far worse adoption quagmires. She shrugged, admitting, "It happens."

Another pause. "Does Candace Wright have any legal rights to William?"

Good question, Michelle thought. "Only if she is the egg donor, as well, and that's not the case in ninety-eight percent of the surrogate arrangements these days." Thad gave her a quizzical look, prompting her to continue explaining. "When the surrogate is also the biological mother, it's literally her child, too, in a purely physical sense, and that mutual DNA complicates how she feels about giving the baby up at birth. So these days, a donor egg, as well as donor sperm, is generally used—the surrogate is simply a host. That makes it a lot easier for the surrogate to surrender the baby at birth."

Thad took that in. "So if that was the arrangement…" he said eventually.

"Then Candace Wright has no legal right or responsibility to the child. The egg donor would also have terminated her legal rights to the baby before implantation, just as your brother did. However, she could be in a position now to reverse that and make a claim on William if no one else wants him." Michelle sighed. "And right now we have no idea who the egg-donor-slash-William's-biological-mother is. But either the Johnsons or Candace Wright will probably know that."

"How do you know so much about surrogate arrangements?"

"Two reasons." Michelle felt a give in the lock she was still trying to undo. "It's now an essential part of family law. And I handled a contract for a client."

Thad's eyes lit with renewed interest. "Did it turn out all right?"

Michelle nodded. "That one went without a hitch. But it was a different situation. The surrogate was the wife's sister. A medical condition prevented the wife from carrying a pregnancy to term, but they were able to use the egg and sperm of the husband and wife, so it was all pretty clear."

Silence fell. Thad looked increasingly conflicted. Michelle's heart went out to him. This was a very tough situation.

"One way or another, I am sure William will find a very good home with loving parents." *She would see to it.*

Thad nodded, his handsome face a mask of sheer male determination. "Initially, I was going to try to track down Candace Wright by phone. Now, I'm thinking our conversation should be done face-to-face."

"I agree," Michelle said. "And you should probably take William—and someone else with you—to witness the events. Just in case there are any questions later about what was said and by whom. It also might be a good idea to get Candace to give you a copy of her original surrogate contract, as well as an affidavit relinquishing any claim to custody, under the current conditions of William's abandonment, if that is still her desire."

"We couldn't just use the letter she left on my front porch?" Thad asked hopefully.

"We'll produce it as evidence of course, but a judge is going to want to see more than that."

"It'll have to go to court?"

"Eventually, yes, because we're talking about a change in whatever custody agreement was put in place prior to William's birth."

Thad exhaled. "This is getting complicated."

Michelle offered a sympathetic smile. "Surrogate arrangements always are." People were rarely prepared for the complexities involved.

"I'm beginning to think I should take legal counsel with us."

Michelle felt another give in the lock. Almost there.

"It's not a bad idea."

From the other room, they heard a whimper, then a full-throated cry. Thad disappeared. When he returned, William was snuggled against his chest, quietly looking around. Michelle could see Thad was already getting his hopes up that the baby would end up staying a member of his family. She didn't want to see him disappointed.

"Will you go with us?" Thad asked.

Aside from Michelle's law partner, Glenn York, there was only one family-law attorney in Summit. Tucker James was a good guy, but not one inclined to work weekends or take on matters that were unusually complex. If this situation turned out to be as messed up as it appeared, Michelle knew Thad was going to need a top-notch attorney experienced in surrogate arrangements. That would be Glenn. Unfortunately Glenn was already working all weekend on a messy divorce-and-property-settlement case that would be in deposition next week. Reluctantly Michelle volunteered. "I can help you out *temporarily.*"

Thad smiled his relief, putting far too much stock in her abilities. "That would be great!"

"One thing, though," Michelle cautioned.

He waited, sandy eyebrows raised.

"No more kissing," she said firmly.

"Agreed." He grinned. "Unless you change your mind."

Oh, how she wanted to, Michelle thought. It had been so

long since she had felt so wanted. So long since her body had hummed with distinctly female satisfaction.

But Thad did not need to know that, she schooled herself sternly.

She looked him in the eye. "I won't."

He went very still. Looking disappointed, but no less determined, she noted.

"Because...?" His low voice sent shivers over her body.

Once again Michelle pushed away the desire welling up inside her. She called on her cool-as-ice courtroom demeanor. "We're neighbors and we need to stay on good terms."

He searched her eyes with daunting intimacy. "And you think we wouldn't if we kissed again?"

I think I'd be devastated if I turned out to be one of your three-dates-and-it's-over women. Hence, better safe than sorry, Michelle thought, as she gave the lock one more nudge. It opened with a click. She lifted the lid. Inside were several insurance policies on expensive camera equipment Russell Garner owned, an old driver's license of his and a Summit High School class ring. There were no legal documents of any kind. Certainly nothing pertaining to a surrogate arrangement.

"I don't know where else to look," Thad said in frustration.

Michelle knew it wasn't the end of the road for getting the information he needed. Far from it. "The attorney who prepared the documents will have copies. Maybe we can find out who that is tomorrow," Michelle said.

Aware her reason for sticking around was gone, she stood. It was as difficult as she'd suspected it would be to leave the baby she had cared for all day. She forced herself to suppress her own deep longing for a child and look at Thad.

"What time did you want to leave tomorrow?" she asked casually.

"Seven in the morning okay with you?"

Michelle held Thad's gaze a moment longer, then touched William's cheek gently. "I'll see you both then."

MICHELLE HAD JUST changed into her pajamas and climbed into bed when the phone rang. Seeing it was Thad, she picked up the receiver and heard the loud, angry wails of an unhappy newborn.

"What's going on?" she asked, aware William hadn't cried that way when she'd been in charge.

More loud crying. "Help," Thad said over the din.

Michelle was already reaching for her slippers. "I'll be right there."

Grabbing her light raincoat, she slipped it on against the chill of the spring evening and headed across the street. Thad was waiting for her, the wailing baby in his arms.

"What's the matter?" Michelle asked, stepping inside.

The moment she spoke, the crying dimmed.

"You poor baby," she soothed.

The wailing stopped altogether.

William studied her with his long-lashed, baby-blue eyes.

"Is it possible he just wanted to hear your voice?" Thad said.

Michelle scoffed and shook her head. "I only wish I were that wonderful. So what's going on?"

"I was trying to give him his formula." Thad pointed to the full bottle on the table next to the sofa.

Michelle walked over and picked it up. She frowned. "It's cold, Thad."

He looked even more clueless. "Yeah, so?"

"You're supposed to heat it."

He held up a hand in expert fashion. "Actually that's an old wives' tale. Infants are perfectly capable of taking their formula cold."

Michelle narrowed her eyes at Thad. "Did they teach you that in medical school?"

"As a matter of fact," he told her smugly, "they did."

Unfortunately, Michelle thought, babies had individual quirks and preferences, just like adults. "Well, maybe that would be okay if he'd had it cold from the beginning. But he hasn't. I gave him warm formula all day. The bottle you gave him earlier this evening was warmed, too."

Thad appeared to think that over, but in the end refused to give ground. "Maybe he just missed you and wants *you* to give him his bottle again."

Michelle's ego liked the idea of that. Her maternal side had other ideas. "And maybe he just wants it warm."

Thad shrugged. "One way to find out." He handed William to Michelle.

She sat down in a chair, her raincoat still on.

His mouth quirked in barely suppressed amusement. "You can take off your coat and stay a while."

No way, she thought. She was in her pj's. No underwear. "I'm fine." Michelle settled William in her arms and offered him the nipple. He looked at her with absolute trust, started to suck, then got a taste of the cold formula. He pushed it out with his tongue and kept looking at Michelle.

"He's not crying," Thad noted.

That was because he was busy snuggling against the softness of her breasts, the way he had all day. Michelle continued making eye contact with the little cutie. It was odd how much she had missed him, so quickly. It wasn't as if he were *her* baby.

Perhaps she should remember that.

Aware Thad was still holding on to his med-school theory about not needing to warm baby formula, Michelle told him wryly, "The only reason he's not crying over cold milk is he's probably wondering how I got so dumb so fast. Right, little fella?"

William's tiny mouth opened slightly. He looked as if he wanted to talk, wanted to tell her what was on his mind, but just couldn't figure out how.

Michelle smiled, utterly besotted.

"Try the bottle again," Thad said.

Knowing a point had to be made here, Michelle did.

William took a taste, then again pushed the bottle away with his lips and tongue. Michelle tried once more. William once more refused it. "I think we should warm it," she reiterated.

"One problem." Thad walked toward the rear of the house. She followed with William and the bottle. Unlike her kitchen, his hadn't been upgraded in many years. The cabinets were painted white, and the walls were covered with a yellow-orange-and-brown-plaid wallpaper. A yellow-laminate-topped breakfast set with padded vinyl chairs were so retro they were back in fashion. The appliances were similarly dated. Even the faded yellow curtain above the sink looked like it had been there since his mother was alive. The only new items in the kitchen were a toaster and a matching coffeemaker.

"I don't know how to warm a bottle," Thad continued.

"Let me guess. You've never done any babysitting, either."

"I've been around kids."

"Not the same thing."

"Apparently not," he conceded.

The silence was contentious. And veering dangerously toward flirtation again. It made her nervous. "Are you paying attention?" she asked.

"Close attention."

Okay, so he still desired her as much as she desired him. It didn't mean they were going to act on it. She gave him the bottle.

Their fingers brushed. She felt the heat of his body all the way to her toes. Swallowed. "Actually, maybe you should do this," she told him. "That way it will be easier for you to remember."

All business now, he said, "Okay."

"They make bottle warmers, but we don't have one, so we're going to do it the old-fashioned way. There was a pretty bowl here earlier…"

"That belongs to Violet Hunter."

Why was Michelle not surprised?

"She brought me some chili in it earlier in the week and I keep forgetting to take it back. She called after you left, offering to come by and get it tonight, but I told her I'd bring it to her at the hospital. Now, if you want me to go out to my car and get it…"

Michelle shook her head. Best he return the bowl to the lovesick nurse as soon as possible. "Where do you keep your bowls?"

He opened a cupboard, revealing a mismatched assortment of dishes, and handed one over.

Michelle shook her head. "That's a cereal bowl. It's way too shallow." She paused. "Surely you've got mixing bowls."

Thad gave her the blank look of a man who did not know his way around a kitchen. Michelle tried a simpler approach. "Where do you keep your pots and pans?"

This he knew. He pointed to a lower cabinet.

Michelle handed William to Thad and knelt to see what was there. Plenty, as it turned out, although again, everything there was at least thirty years old. She took out a saucepan, carried it to the sink and filled it with very warm tap water. She set the bottle in the pan, so the water covered the contents.

Thad leaned in, over her shoulder. "And now?"

"We wait."

Thad edged closer, smiling down at the baby. "How will

we know when the bottle's the right temperature?" he asked as he and the baby made goo-goo eyes at each other.

"We'll keep testing it. It should only take a few minutes."

"Hear that, William?" Thad gently caressed the little one's cheek. "Your dinner will be ready shortly."

Three minutes later, the formula was the right temperature. They returned to the living room.

Thad sat down to give William his bottle. William made a face and pushed the nipple right back out.

"*Now* what's wrong?" Thad asked.

Michelle could only guess. "Maybe William senses you're uncertain."

Thad didn't deny that could be the problem. "Maybe you should give it a try again," he said.

Figuring the little one had waited long enough for his feeding, Michelle sat down next to Thad on the sofa. He handed the baby to her. She shifted William so he was in a semi-upright position, resting in the crook of her arm. "We know you're hungry," she said, putting the nipple to his lips. William just stared at her, still refusing to drink. "You're not going to be able to go back to sleep until you take this bottle," Michelle said softly, gently rubbing the nipple back and forth across his lips. "So give it a try, little guy."

Still watching her, William opened his mouth, took the nipple and began to suck. Twenty minutes and two burps later, William had downed all three ounces.

"I guess he was hungry," Thad mused.

Reluctantly Michelle handed the baby back to him. She knew she shouldn't be getting this involved in something that was essentially not her problem, but she really wished she could stay right here with the two of them, or better yet, take William home with her.

Reminding herself that was not an option, Michelle stood. "He should be good for three hours," she said.

"Sure you don't want to stay the night? We could have a slumber party."

The image of Thad in his pj's was all she needed to throw her overheated senses into overdrive. She quickened her pace. "Nice try."

William in his arms, he followed her into the foyer. "What should I do if he starts crying again?"

Michelle paused, her hand on the doorknob. "Generally speaking, if William is unhappy, it's one of four things—he's wet, hungry, sleepy or in need of comfort and reassurance. Just go down the list, and if all else fails, just talk to him."

Thad said, a tender note in his tone, "He likes your voice."

And I like yours, Michelle thought, realizing how easily she could get used to being around Thad.

She smiled. "He'll like yours, too, if he hears it often enough."

"Thanks for coming over." Thad shot her a look full of gratitude. "For helping. For everything."

Unwillingly Michelle flashed back to another man, another time, and gratitude that had been mistaken for something else. She hardened her defenses, knowing she had to be careful. "Try to get some sleep." She opened the door.

"Can I call you in an emergency?" he asked as Michelle swept into the darkness of the cloudy spring night.

She nodded, throwing the words over her shoulder. "But *only* if it's an emergency."

MICHELLE HALF EXPECTED Thad to call her every three hours through the night. He didn't. Several times she got up and went to the window and looked across the street to his home. At eleven, two and five, the lights were on, and the rest of the time the house was dark. Which probably meant, she thought, that William was sleeping between feedings.

Telling herself that was good—Thad could easily handle parenting William on his own, after all—Michelle forced herself to go back to bed each time and try to get some sleep.

When the alarm went off at six, it was a relief. She skipped her usual morning run and headed for the shower. At seven, Thad and William were at her door.

Soon after, they were off, Michelle and Thad sitting in the front of his BMW SUV, William sleeping contentedly in the middle of the rear seat.

"So how was your night?" Michelle asked, opening up her briefcase. If she was going to protect her heart, she needed to stay in business mode.

"Fine, as soon as William and I reached an understanding."

Michelle heard the smile in Thad's voice. "And that was?"

"There was only one place he was going to sleep more than ten minutes."

She sent him a sidelong glance. "You held him all night?"

Thad nodded, looking as content as she had felt after spending all day holding William. "I slept in the reading chair and ottoman in the study, and he slept on my chest."

Michelle could imagine that was a very warm and snuggly place to sleep. She cast a look back at William, but couldn't see a lot, because the infant seat was facing backward. "I'm surprised he's been content in his car seat for as long as he has."

"It's probably the motion," Thad theorized.

As it turned out, he was probably right. William slept all the way to Big Spring, and continued sleeping as they followed the MapQuest directions to the address listed for Candace Wright.

The surrogate mother lived in a small yellow bungalow with

a sparse lawn and overgrown shrubbery. "Think one of us should ring the bell and see if she's home first?" Michelle asked.

Before Thad could reply, the front door opened and a slightly pudgy young woman stepped out. Arms crossed in front of her, her long dishwater-blond hair whipping around in the spring breeze, she stalked over to the car. Took a glance at the infant seat in back. Sighed. "Let's not do this on the street," she said, motioning at the bungalow.

THAD WASN'T SURE what he expected the surrogate mother's home to be like. Certainly not a wall-to-wall artist's studio, with beautiful landscapes stacked against every surface, and an easel with a half-finished canvas front and center in the room.

"I'm sorry I had to leave the baby like that," Candace Wright said as soon as introductions had been made, "but I was afraid you'd be like everyone else in this mess and refuse to take him."

"You're sure Brice and Beatrix Johnson don't want him, either?" Michelle asked.

"Apparently not." Clearly confused about the situation, Candace shrugged. "I'm as surprised as you are. They were thrilled about the baby until a couple of days before William was born. Then they started acting a little weird, almost like they were having second thoughts."

"Did you ask them about that?" Thad interrupted.

Candace shook her head. "I told myself they were just nervous about becoming parents. Happens to a lot of people, from what I've seen. Anyway, they came to the hospital and were there when William was born. As soon as they held him they seemed really happy again. We signed the papers. They took him home. Everything was great. A day later, Beatrix shows up at my door with the baby, completely distraught, and just hands him to me."

Thad and Michelle both did a double take, but it was Michelle who asked the question first. "With no explanation?"

Candace lifted her hands in helpless frustration. "Beatrix said a lot of things, but none of it made any sense, she was crying so hard. All I got out of her was that she couldn't do this right now…and maybe not ever…and that because I was his mom I had to take care of baby William…there was no one else. By then he was crying, too. Beatrix really started sobbing." Candace sighed and shoved a hand through her hair. "Beatrix mumbled something about her husband needing her, then she ran back to the car, jumped in and drove off, still crying her eyes out. I didn't know what was going on, so I called the lady lawyer who handled the legal stuff for the surrogate arrangement—"

"Do you have her card?"

Candace nodded and went to retrieve it. "She sounded as stunned as I was when I told her what had just happened, but she wouldn't do anything, or even talk about the situation with me."

"She really couldn't until she had spoken to her clients," Michelle explained.

"That doesn't make sense!" Candace complained.

"It's complicated," Michelle admitted. "But her first duty, as the Johnsons' legal counsel, is to them. Whatever is said to her is privileged and can't be shared with anyone else without their express permission. Otherwise, she could be disbarred."

"Whatever!" Candace scowled. "Anyway, she said she'd have to investigate and get back to me. I asked her to come and get the baby. She said not until she spoke to her clients. And then she asked me to sit tight and take care of the baby until other arrangements could be made." The young woman threw up her hands in exasperation. "I've got a showing in Houston next month. I'm already way behind in what I need to have ready, and I don't have time for this! So then I remembered that Russell had said he had a brother who was a doctor in Summit, Texas. I looked you up on the Internet, got your address and dropped William off and ran before you could tell me you didn't want the responsibility for him, either. Not that any of this was supposed to be my problem, anyway. I only agreed to be a surrogate so I could afford to stay home for a year and concentrate on my art! I never wanted to become a parent. I *still* don't."

Thad wasn't sure whether to be grateful or annoyed that the surrogate was so emotionally distanced from William.

"What about the donor egg? Do you know where that came from?" Michelle asked.

Candace nodded. "There was a nurse the Johnsons knew at the fertility clinic. She felt sorry for them just like I did because they wanted a kid so bad, and it wasn't going to happen for them any other way. She's the one who donated the egg."

"Do you have the nurse's name?"

Candace sobered. "She died in a boating accident a couple months ago."

"Did she have family?" Michelle asked.

"No." Candace paused. "So that just leaves Russell as William's family. Since I can't find Russell, that means you have to deal with this, Dr. Garner! Because I can't! And frankly," she finished wearily, "I shouldn't have to, since I was just the vessel that carried the baby. Nothing more."

MICHELLE AND THAD STAYED long enough to get an affidavit from Candace briefly explaining what had happened.

Michelle telephoned the San Angelo attorney who had handled the private surrogate arrangement and left a message, asking to meet with her as soon as possible. And then Michelle and Thad headed toward the Johnson home in San Angelo, William in tow.

Unlike Candace Wright's humble artist's lair, Brice and Beatrix Johnson lived in a very nice home that sat on several acres of land in an exclusive gated community. Thad drove up the paved drive and, as before, they'd barely gotten out of Thad's SUV when the front door opened. A woman Thad estimated to be in her early forties rushed out, overnight bag in hand. Her hair was wet—as if she had just gotten out of the shower and hadn't taken time to dry it. The little bit of makeup she did have on could not hide her red nose or the fragile puffiness surrounding her red-rimmed eyes. She stopped when she saw the baby cradled in Thad's arms. Her expression fell.

Thad took a chance. "Beatrix?"

She nodded, eyes still on little William.

Thad extended his free hand. "I'm Thad Garner, Russell Garner's brother. This is my attorney, Michelle Anderson. We need to talk."

As Thad had hoped, Beatrix Johnson acquiesced. Minutes later, they were all settled in the elegant white living room. Briefly, Thad explained how they came to have custody of William.

Beatrix continued to look a little shell-shocked. "I'm so sorry. This is all such a mess."

"So you have changed your mind about adopting William?" Thad asked.

Beatrix nodded, looking all the more miserable but no less resolute.

Michelle pulled a notepad from her bag and began to take notes. "And you started having doubts a few days before William was born?"

Beatrix reached for a tissue. If she was surprised at how much they knew, she didn't show it. "We found out I was pregnant—with twins. Due in six months. At first we were just so stunned. We didn't know if we would be able to handle three children born so close together, but then we decided we could."

William stirred and Thad cradled the baby closer to his chest. "So you took him home from the hospital."

Beatrix nodded. Fleeting happiness appeared on her face. "It seemed like everything was going to be fine." She paused for a breath and her expression changed. "And then the very next day my husband was in a terrible car accident. So I rushed the baby over to Candace and I went to the hospital to be with my husband and that's where I've been ever since. I just came home this morning to shower and get a fresh change of clothing. I was on my way back to see Brice when you arrived."

"Is your husband going to be all right?" Thad asked.

Beatrix's shoulders slumped in obvious relief. "The doctors think so, but he has a broken back and leg and months of re-habilitation ahead of him." Beatrix's lower lip trembled. "I can't handle a newborn, take care of my husband and be pregnant with twins at the same time. Even if we were to get help in, it's just too much!" She dabbed at her eyes. "I talked to my husband this morning. And as much as it breaks our hearts, he agrees. We have to do what is right for William and find him a home where he can get the love and attention he deserves."

MICHELLE WAITED until the three of them had stopped for lunch at a park on the outskirts of town before she asked Thad, "Are you okay? You've had a lot to try to absorb the past thirty hours or so."

Thad walked William back and forth while she added powdered formula to sun-warmed bottled water. His expression as sober as his thoughts, he turned his gaze back to hers and told her what was on his mind. "My brother's attitude I can almost understand. Russell likes to help people on the fly, and he never thinks things through. Candace Wright obviously needs money, and I think her heart is in the right place, too. She could have turned the baby over to foster care, or driven to the closest police or fire station and dropped him off there anonymously." He exhaled. "Instead, she drove him all the way to Summit and left him with me. With the only true family William has."

"You're right." Michelle shook the bottle vigorously. "The surrogate mother could have simply called 9-1-1 and let them sort it out. As for Brice and Beatrix Johnson—" This wasn't anything they had asked for. "They're really in a tough spot. My heart goes out to them."

Thad accepted the bottle she gave him. Still standing, he offered it to William and watched as the little boy began to take the formula. "I feel for them, too," Thad said. "This is a very difficult situation. Clearly, it's not easy for them to give the little guy up, but they are forcing themselves to be realistic, no matter how much it hurts, and do what is best for William under the circumstances. They're putting him first. Just as I intend to do."

Michelle caught her breath at the intent look in Thad's eyes. Although she wasn't supposed to be getting emotionally involved, this was what she had secretly hoped for. "What are you saying, Thad?" she asked cautiously, needing to be sure.

Thad stepped closer yet, steely determination in his golden-brown eyes. "I want to adopt William, Michelle." Deliberately, Thad held her gaze. "Will you help me?"

Chapter Four

"I know you mean well."

He guided her to the low brick wall that edged the grass surrounding the picnic area. Making sure they were out of earshot of everyone else, he sat down with William still in his arms and stretched his legs out in front of him. "But…?"

Michelle sat down, too, making sure there was a good distance between them. Which he promptly closed, simply by sliding toward her. "Adopting a child is not like helping out in an emergency. It's a lifelong commitment."

"You think I don't understand that?" He sounded faintly annoyed.

She turned so her bent knee was touching his rock-hard thigh. "I think you're acting in the heat of emotion because you feel responsible for this child in a way no one else seems to, and because you've grown to care for him." And it wasn't hard to see why. William was a very lovable little boy, cute and fragile in the way all newborn babies were.

"I'm not going to change my mind."

If he had other children or even a wife, Michelle might feel differently. But he was a bachelor, a man who'd never been able to settle on one woman. She sent him a level look, aware her heart was racing again. "You need to think about this," she insisted.

His voice dropped. "I have thought about it—all last night and today."

So had Michelle.

But five years' experience in family law had taught her to proceed cautiously. Decisions made in the heat of emotion were often the wrong ones. "I know this seems like a good idea now," she said gently, determined to remain sensible, "but you've only been responsible for William for the past thirty-some hours, and of that time, I was taking care of him for thirteen hours."

He acknowledged this with a slight nod of his head, his eyes never leaving hers. "I had him by myself all last night."

She pretended she wasn't playing with fire here. "And had help from me again today. What's going to happen when you and I both have to go to work tomorrow?"

He lifted his broad shoulders in an unapologetic shrug. "I'm off tomorrow and I traded my Tuesday shift, which means I don't work again until Wednesday. That gives me time to figure something out, after I get the legal issues taken care of."

Michelle tried not to make too much of his unexpectedly bold confession. She swallowed the knot of emotion in her throat. "You're really getting ahead of yourself here, Thad." Ignoring the warmth in Thad's eyes as he gave William his bottle, she said, "Brice and Beatrix Johnson haven't officially terminated their rights yet."

Thad waited until William had a good ounce, then handed her the bottle and moved William to his shoulder for a burp. As he patted the infant gently on the back, he said, "They will."

He was so confident.

Michelle's gaze drifted to the trusting way William rested his cheek on Thad's shoulder, his angelic face turned into the comforting curve of Thad's neck. They were so cute together, these two Garner guys, already looking so much like father and son.

"As far as the law is concerned, right now Brice and Beatrix Johnson are still William's parents. You have physical custody of the child *only* because they are allowing it."

Thad shifted William back into the strong cradle of his arms and offered the bottle again. Michelle watched as William suckled eagerly. It was as if at some point during the night the infant had decided he wanted Thad to be his family as much as Thad wanted William to be his.

"What do you think I should do next then—from a practical standpoint?" Thad asked.

"Get legal representation for yourself as soon as possible." More a friend now than counsel, Michelle put a gentle hand on his arm and looked him in the eye. "And in the meantime, you need to really think about this tonight, Thad. And make absolutely certain it's what you want to do." *Before you and William bond even more...*

"THAD GARNER is on the line. He wants an appointment ASAP."

Michelle had already alerted Becky—her and Glenn's legal secretary—that Thad might be calling. She'd also talked to Glenn about the situation. "Ask him if he can come in at nine-thirty."

Becky relayed the information, then covered the mouthpiece. "He wants to know if it's okay if he brings the baby."

Trying not to think how much she had missed seeing William during the night, Michelle nodded. "Of course."

An hour later Thad arrived.

Michelle knew he was there, because she could hear Becky oohing and ahhing even before he was formally announced.

Seconds later Thad walked in. He was wearing a light blue button-down shirt and khaki dress pants. He looked every bit the doting father, with William bundled up in his arms. He aimed a smile her way. "Good morning."

It was *now,* Michelle thought. She slipped back into a business frame of mind and returned calmly, "Good morning,"

Looking as glad to see her as she was to see him, Thad walked over and transferred the baby to her arms. "William wants to say hello to you," he told her softly.

Michelle looked down at the sweetly composed little face. "He's asleep," she noted dryly.

Thad's husky voice broke the silence of the room. He sat on the edge of her desk. "Not for long, if the current trend continues."

Michelle rocked back in her swivel chair. It felt so good having the little fellow in her arms again. Longing swept through her. If only he could be *her* child. "Long night?"

He traded glances with her, heaved a rueful sigh. "I couldn't put him down for more than ten minutes at a time without him waking and wanting to be held." Thad lifted a palm. "I know what the old hands at child-rearing would say, but…I don't think he could be spoiled yet. Do you?"

Michelle looked down at William. No way was this angel spoiled! "I imagine he's just trying to figure out where he fits in this world."

"Well, I know with whom." A mixture of determination and protectiveness laced Thad's low tone.

"Meaning?" she asked.

"I haven't changed my mind," Thad told her. "I still want to proceed with what we talked about yesterday afternoon."

"All right, then." Michelle reluctantly handed William back to Thad and pressed the intercom button. "Becky, would you please ask Glenn to come in."

Moments later Michelle's former law-school colleague and new law partner strode in. The thirty-four-year-old father had a mild-mannered look that was deceptive; he was an extremely effective litigator, and an even more acclaimed negotiator with a reputation for crafting solutions that made everyone happy, even in the messiest divorces and custody cases. The two of them had joined forces several months before to buy out two retiring Summit lawyers and take over their practice.

Like her, Glenn—and his family—were new to that area of Texas. "As I told you yesterday, Glenn does all the family-law cases for our firm. I'm going to meet with the two of you long enough to bring him up to speed, and then he'll be happy to help you."

To MICHELLE'S RELIEF, Thad did not press her to represent him but, instead, took the assignment of counsel graciously. She excused herself and headed to court. From there, she went to a meeting with a client, back to court for another hearing on a business dispute she was handling, and then back to the office to draft a will for yet another client.

Only when she had finished did she pack up and head home for the day. When she reached her street, she could not say she was all that surprised to see balloons tied to the mailbox, a big wooden stork sign and at least two dozen cars parked on the drive and on either side of the street. Thad Garner was having a party. Whether or not it was premature was too soon to tell.

Glad she hadn't received an update from Glenn regarding

the progress of Thad's case but, instead, had stuck to her own clients' needs, Michelle grabbed her briefcase and headed into the house. She'd barely had time to kick off her shoes when the doorbell rang. Through the beveled glass in the front door she could see a familiar figure. She went to answer it.

Looking as happy as any father coming out of the delivery room, Thad handed her a bubblegum cigar.

"Celebrate with us," he urged.

Michelle lifted her eyebrows. "I don't know. Sort of looks like you have your hands full."

Doubtless Violet Hunter was there, too.

Not that she was jealous.

Thad clamped a cigar between his teeth. "It's a hand-me-down shower. Everyone brought stuff their kids no longer need." Sensing correctly that stronger persuasion was needed, he lounged against the portal. "Seriously, it's a lot of fun. And there are a lot of people from the hospital I'd like you to meet."

Michelle didn't deny she needed to get acquainted with more people in the community. In the three months she'd been in Summit, she'd been so busy working and meeting with clients, she'd had no time for socializing.

She tried to sound casual. "Where's William?"

Thad's mouth curved in a playful smile. "Back at the house, greeting his adoring friends and neighbors."

Did she really want to miss that, too? "What's the dress code?" she asked.

"Come as you are." He took her hand, drawing her close. "Which means you can come as you are."

In a suit and heels? She tugged back. "I'd prefer to change."

Impatience underscored his low tone. "Promise you won't take long?"

She fell victim to the seductive smile. "Five minutes."

"I'm going to hold you to that," Thad murmured with another lingering look, then he released her hand and headed out the front door.

IT WAS FIFTEEN minutes. Thad knew, because he was watching the clock and the door. The wait was worth it, though, when Michelle walked into the party.

She had changed into a pale yellow, V-necked sweater, black denim jeans and boots that made the most of her long and lean runner's body. She'd swept up a section of her gorgeous hair in a jeweled clasp. Her cheeks were flushed pink. From self-consciousness? he wondered. Interesting, because he'd never seen her ill at ease before. Unless you counted the aftermath of their one and only kiss. Then, she had looked much the same way. As if she'd wanted to be with him, and she didn't. As if she'd enjoyed kissing him, yet wished she hadn't fallen victim to the potent chemistry sizzling between them.

"You made it." Thad wrapped an arm around her shoulders and guided her into the throng of curious coworkers. "Let me introduce you to everyone…"

To Thad's satisfaction, Michelle warmed to the throng as much as they warmed to her. She especially hit it off with Dotty Pederson, which was good, Thad thought.

"Dotty has agreed to be William's nanny," he told Michelle.

Out of the corner of his eye, Thad could see Violet Hunter watching the two of them, an inscrutable expression on her normally cheerful countenance.

At the same time, Michelle looked as if she didn't know whether to be happy or concerned about Dotty Pederson's new position in William's life. Not sure why she'd object to the hiring of a nanny, Thad continued, "Dotty used to supervise the E.R. nursing staff. She retired last summer."

Dotty ran a hand through her short, white hair. A smile split her elfin face. "I'm sixty. It was time. But I've been bored, staying at home. This will be perfect, especially since Thad has agreed to let me care for William in my home while he's working at the E.R."

Beside him, Thad felt Michelle relax ever so slightly. "That does sound perfect," she said.

Still, Thad could see that something about the arrangement was bugging her. And he was even more sure of it when she slipped off toward the buffet table seconds later and lost herself in the throng.

By eight-thirty the impromptu party was winding down.

Guests began departing. When Michelle looked as if she was about to head for the door, too, Thad brought William to her. "Mind holding the little guy for a few minutes?" Thad said. He put William in Michelle's arms before she could formulate a reply.

That was all it took. Michelle melted visibly at the sight and feel of the baby in her arms. She looked, Thad thought, like a natural-born mother.

The kind every kid would want and should have. And the kind William needed.

MICHELLE WASN'T fooled. She knew Thad had asked her to hold William in order to make sure she was the last guest to depart. She couldn't really say she minded. She hadn't had a chance to cuddle William since this morning at the law office, and she had missed him. And Thad. Which was ridiculous. She and Thad barely knew each other!

"So how are things going?" she asked Thad as soon as they were alone. She still wanted to stay uninvolved, but figured a few more minutes' conversation with Thad wouldn't hurt anything.

Thad put the plastic cups and paper plates in plastic garbage bags. "Glenn didn't tell you?"

Michelle swayed a surprisingly wide-awake William back and forth. "I haven't seen him. Although for the record, he probably won't keep me apprised of what's going on unless I'm called in, in a pinch, to handle something on the case."

Thad frowned. "I'm not sure I like that." He bent over to put a twist tie on the bag, then set it in the laundry room, just inside the back door. Then he rummaged beneath the sink and pulled out a roll of paper towels and some disinfectant cleaner. He spritzed the sticky places on the counter, then rubbed them dry with a paper towel. "Don't get me wrong. Glenn is a nice guy and he seems very competent."

"He is."

Finished, Thad wadded up the paper towel and threw it in the trash can beneath the sink. "I'll just feel better if you're involved, on some level." He turned to face her. "So what I want to ask you is this—will you sit in on all the lawyer-client meetings and conference calls, not as cocounsel, since you're clearly uncomfortable with that, but as my friend?"

THAD DIDN'T KNOW what Michelle's reaction was going to be. He knew what he wanted—her by his side. And not just in legal meetings or court hearings. Or for William's sake. But for his.

"Have you talked to Glenn about this?" Michelle asked finally.

Thad lounged against the counter, arms folded. "I asked him if he would mind if you remained involved on some level, and he didn't. So…will you be there as my friend?"

Michelle raked her teeth across her lower lip. "I guess you don't have anyone else you'd rather ask?"

Unsure how blunt to be, Thad said, "I trust you." *I want*

you. "William trusts you. I just think you'd be a good person to be on our team."

She smiled faintly, then finally relented. "All right," she said. "I'll be there whenever the two of you need me."

Gratitude flooded through him. "Thank you."

Michelle crossed to him and settled against the counter next to him, so the wide-awake William could see both of them at the same time. "So bring me up to speed on what happened in your meeting with Glenn," she suggested.

"He contacted Beatrix and Brice Johnson's attorney while I was in the office. Their attorney confirmed that the Johnsons did want to terminate their parental rights, and since my petition-slash-motion to adopt has to be filed at the same time, they decided Glenn would file all the papers simultaneously with the court as soon as he gets the signed and notarized affidavits from the other attorney." He paused. "He's supposed to get them tomorrow morning and file everything with family court by the end of business tomorrow."

"Wow." Michelle looked impressed.

"I know. I'm pleased with how fast it's all happening, too."

She shifted to better see his face. "No second thoughts?"

Sensing she would understand, Thad confided, "I admit I'm a little overwhelmed with the logistics of becoming a parent, all the stuff that has to be done, but I feel good about having Dotty babysit William when I'm at work. She's an excellent nurse, as well as a mother and grandmother, so he'll be in good hands. And I had a lot of others volunteer to help out, too, so I know I've got the child care covered." He sighed. "The only thing that really bothers me is the waiting period, after the papers are filed with the court. Glenn said it could take thirty to forty-five days before we get a hearing and the adoption becomes final." Thad frowned, wanting Michelle's reaction. "It seems like a long time to wait."

She didn't seem to think so. "Why?"

Thad tensed. "I guess I worry someone else will come forward and want William, too. Or Brice and Beatrix will change their minds." And that would really suck.

Michelle raised her face to his. "What about you?" she said softly, searching his eyes. "Is there any chance *you'll* change your mind?"

It was an innocent question, bluntly put. Thad wasn't offended. Maybe because he knew she was only asking because she had come to care for William and wanted to see the little guy loved and protected as much as he did. "Not a chance," he said.

Michelle smiled.

"So," Thad continued, "will you be my backup on this?" *Legally and...otherwise?*

Michelle took the hand he offered. "It would be an honor," she said.

HAPPY EVERYTHING was working out for Thad and William so quickly and so well, Michelle gave William a bath and a bottle and rocked him in the rocker-glider someone had brought to the shower, while Thad took out the trash and finished cleaning up after the impromptu party.

By the time he had finished, William was asleep in her arms.

Thad carried the bassinet someone else had given him upstairs and placed it next to the bed in the master bedroom.

Michelle laid the snoozing William on his back in the cozy infant bed. He jerked his arms and legs. She placed her hand gently on his tummy, reassuring him. His movements quieted.

Acutely aware of Thad standing beside her, she stayed there a moment longer, then backed soundlessly out of the room and headed down the stairs beside him.

The house was quiet.

So quiet she could hear the meter of their breaths.

At the foot of the stairs she stopped and looked up at him. He looked down at her. The next thing she knew she was in his arms. His lips were on hers. And the world around them ground to a halt as emotion built upon emotion.

She wasn't sure what drew her more, the fact that Thad was such a decent guy or that he knew how to kiss like no one else.

One touch of his lips and she was on fire. The sweep of his tongue was even more electric. He tasted hot and male and possessed her with a kiss so intimate and sure she tingled all over. Wanted all the more. And did not know, for the first time in a very long time, if she ever wanted to stop.

THAD HADN'T MEANT to kiss her tonight, and certainly not like this, with no warning and no restraint. But when she stopped and looked up at him, her breath catching at the same time the air stalled in his chest, he knew it was kiss her then and there, or regret the chance not taken. So he had wrapped his arms around her, drawn her close and lowered his mouth to hers.

And once their lips had touched, there was no question—he had to give it his all. Had to discover again what she liked, how she kissed, how she tasted, at the end of a very long day.

Initially, she simply surrendered to the kiss, let him take the lead. But it wasn't long before she was venturing, too, tangling her tongue with his, increasing the pressure of her lips, opening her mouth to his all the more.

Heat and speed turned to languorous desire for them both. Then sweet, wild yearning. A passion destined to be fulfilled.

And that was when a furious, high-pitched cry split the air, drawing them apart.

"WILLIAM," THEY SAID in unison.

Michelle shook her head. "I can't believe he's awake again."

"Dotty suggested swaddling," Thad said, as the two of them ascended the stairs and headed for the master bedroom.

Michelle tensed. "I've heard of it, of course, but I've never done it."

"I've never done it, either." Thad picked William up and put him against his shoulder. In a replay of what had happened repeatedly over the past two days, as soon as he was picked up, William stopped crying and cuddled against Thad's broad shoulder, deeply content but also wide-awake. Doubtless knowing the lack of quality sleep couldn't be any better for the baby than it was for him, Thad asked, "Think we can find instructions on the Internet?"

"I'm sure we can," Michelle said.

They went into the study down the hall. Thad's computer was already booted up, so it was easy to sit down and do a search.

"Problem number one," Thad said, after they'd perused the instructions. "We don't have a swaddling blanket."

"Are you sure?" Michelle asked him. "You've got those bags of used infant clothing down there. There might be one in there."

"Good point."

"You stay here with William. I'll go look," Michelle said. She returned with two shopping bags full of infant clothing, most of it for newborns, as well as half-a-dozen stretchy, waffle-weave receiving blankets. She held one up for him to peruse. "I think this is what they're talking about."

"Looks right," Thad said.

"Where should we do this?"

Thad shrugged. "My bed?"

Michelle flushed, despite herself. "Good idea."

She led the way into Thad's bedroom. Glad for something

to concentrate on other than the man who slept in this very bed, she spread out the baby blanket on the mattress, then folded down one corner of it. Thad placed William on it, then together they aligned his shoulders with the top of the blanket. Next, they brought one side over and tucked it underneath him, just as the instructions had said.

"Now the other side," Thad murmured.

Last but not least, they brought the bottom point up and tucked it in the hem just under his chin.

William had been patient while all the wrapping was going on. When he realized he could no longer wave his arms and legs, his face scrunched up and he let out another lusty cry.

Michelle picked him up and looked down into his face. "Now, now, this is not so bad. Being swaddled like this is going to help you sleep."

William's lower lip shot out.

Thad laughed.

William looked at Thad, as if wondering what this was all about. Thad looked at Michelle. The two looked so good together. So perfect. Like mother and son.

She handed him over gently. "I think you should rock him now."

Thad frowned. "I'm not sure he's going to go back to sleep. He's had ten minutes."

Michelle gave them both an indulgent look. "I think he will if you rock him."

She was looking for an excuse to leave, Thad thought, before they found themselves alone and started kissing again.

"You just want a good night's sleep," Thad teased.

"Yep." Michelle pranced out of his bedroom and back downstairs.

Thad followed, William in his arms.

Michelle paused in the hallway to kiss William's cheek and look deep into Thad's eyes. "Seriously, I hope this swaddling thing works," she told him.

"I hope so, too," Thad said.

Otherwise it was going to be a long night.

Chapter Five

The next morning, Thad had just finished giving William his nine-o'clock bottle when the doorbell rang. He'd been up for hours. He hadn't had a shower or shaved yet. But maybe that was a good thing, he mused, if his early caller was yet another single woman hoping to rescue him from single fatherhood. Maybe she'd take one look at him and run scared.

Holding William in his arms, football style, he made his way to the door.

Michelle stood on the other side of the threshold. Unlike him, she was dressed for work, in a gray pin-striped suit, silky white blouse and conservative gray heels. A simple silver necklace rested just below her collarbone, in the open V of her blouse. She had her briefcase slung over one shoulder, her BlackBerry in her palm. She finished reading whatever was written on the screen, then looked at him, her expression grave.

Thad's gut tightened. There were times in his life when he kept waiting for the other shoe to drop. This was one of them. "Something up?" he asked casually.

As Michelle nodded, her silky hair brushed against her chin. Her eyes held his. "May I come in?"

"Sure."

Her heels clicking on his wood floors, Michelle followed him into the living room, where the gifts from the impromptu shower were still heaped in messy stacks. Thad knew he should be doing something with all the stuff, but right now he had no idea what to do with most of it. Although a few of the blankets and a couple of baby rattles had already come in handy.

The fragrance of Michelle's hair and skin sending his senses into overdrive, Thad reached down with his free hand and cleared a place for her in a club chair.

She flashed a too-polite smile, then gracefully moved to take the seat. "Glenn's in Fort Stockton this morning taking a deposition for another case, so he asked me to cover for him."

Thad moved past her and sat down on the sofa across from her. "What's happened?"

Michelle's eyes reflected the concern of someone left to deliver bad news.

"We just got word from Family Court," she told him matter-of-factly. "Your case has been assigned to Judge Barnes."

"That's bad, I take it."

Michelle hesitated a second too long for Thad's comfort. "Judge Barnes is something of a stickler."

Meaning, Thad thought, old-fashioned and sexist.

"He's really by-the-book," Michelle continued with obvious reluctance. "And he doesn't mince words. He tends to say exactly what's on his mind."

William snuggled against Thad's chest and, even in his sleep, let out a contented sigh. Thad tore his gaze from the baby's precious face. "And what is on Judge Barnes's mind?" he inquired warily.

Briefly worry lit her pretty green eyes. "We're about to find out. He wants you and William and your representative—

which right now is going to be me—and the Johnsons and their attorney, Karin Hendricks, in his courtroom at 1:00 p.m. today."

"You don't think…" Thad swallowed around the sudden compression in his throat. "He's not going to order William into *foster* care, is he?"

From her inscrutable expression, Thad noticed Michelle wasn't making any promises. "Besides, I thought I didn't have to go to court for thirty to forty-five days."

"Generally, that's the way it works," Michelle allowed.

"But not in this case?"

Michelle tugged down the hem of her skirt, which had ridden up slightly on her thigh. She leaned forward. "There are unusual aspects to the origin of the agreement between you and the Johnsons regarding the adoption, as well as how you came to have physical custody of the child. It's appropriate for Judge Barnes to want to go over everything and make sure everyone is on the same page."

FOUR HOURS LATER Michelle met Thad and William just outside the hearing room in the Summit County Courthouse. Thad looked very handsome in an olive-green suit and tie. William was wearing a white sleeper with a satin yellow duck sewn across the front.

Had Michelle not known better, she would have thought Thad was William's father in every sense. Which made the stakes for this hearing all the higher.

As Michelle expected, Judge Barnes didn't waste any time getting down to the business of the hearing, once he was seated behind the bench. His penetrating stare was as no-nonsense as his close-cropped gray beard and thick, closely shorn hair. Gruffly he made himself known to all parties present, then he slid his black-rimmed bifocals down the bridge of his nose, and spoke to the attorney for the Johnsons. "As discussed, due to Mr. Johnson's hospitalization, I am waiving your clients' appearance today, but next time, I'll expect to have at least Mrs. Johnson present in this courtroom."

"Yes, Your Honor," Karin Hendricks said.

The judge turned to Thad. His assessing gaze rested on the baby cradled in Thad's arms, then he looked at the papers in front of him one last time.

The suspense was almost unbearable.

Finally Judge Barnes frowned and said, "Let's make sure I understand this correctly, Dr. Garner. This baby was left on your doorstep after the adoptive parents changed their minds about adopting him. They gave baby William back to the surrogate mother, and she didn't want responsibility for him, either. The surrogate mother tried to give William back to one Russell Garner, the sperm donor, who also happens to be your brother. She couldn't find your brother, so she left William on your doorstep with a note asking you to take care of the matter, and you've been caring for the little boy for the past three days."

Thad nodded. "That's correct, Your Honor."

"You and the attorney present, Michelle Anderson, have spoken to your brother, Russell, and he does not wish to reverse his prior termination of any and all parental rights to the child."

"That's also correct."

Judge Barnes slid his bifocals even farther down his nose. "And now you think *you* want to adopt him?" Skepticism rang in his voice.

"I don't think—I *know*," Thad said firmly.

Good, rock-solid answer, Michelle thought.

Judge Barnes rocked back in his chair, took off his glasses entirely and set them on the desk in front of him. "Forgive me, son, for being blunt here, but you have no clue what you're getting into. I'm a father myself—and I do! Parenting is hard work, a lifelong commitment, not something you take on as a whim or out of guilt or some misguided sense of family. This would make a lot more sense to me if you were already married and had kids of your own, or at the very least had another family member at home who could help you out. But you don't."

Fearing the judge was about to remand William to foster care, Michelle cut in, "With all due respect, Your Honor, single people *can* foster and adopt."

Judge Barnes picked up his glasses and slid them back on. "Sure they can. When they've thought long and hard about it, and gone through all the proper interviews and home studies." He pointed to the papers in front of him. "None of that has been done here. And while I applaud Dr. Garner for stepping up and trying to do right by this child, in these very unusual circumstances, I also think reacting emotionally is not the solution. Therefore, I'm ordering social services to begin an investigation immediately, starting today. If the social worker assigned believes the home environment is suitable for a newborn, William can stay with Dr. Garner until such time as an adoption petition is considered by this court."

"Thank you, Your Honor," Thad said in obvious relief.

"Don't thank me." Judge Barnes glowered. "Just make sure you consider this carefully and do right by that child."

"You don't have to worry about the social-worker evaluation," Thad told Michelle as she led the way out the rear entrance of the limestone courthouse to the parking lot. "I work with social workers all the time at the hospital. The people in the department know I'm a good guy."

Talk about naive, Michelle thought. Briefcase still in hand, she struggled to keep up with his longer strides. Not easy, considering the narrow hem of her skirt.

She curled a hand around his biceps, wordlessly slowing him down. "This isn't about whether or not you are a good guy, Thad," she told him grimly. "It's about what is best for William. Child Protective Services could easily decide that he would be better off in a home with a mother *and* a father. He's a newborn. There's no shortage of people waiting for a baby—people who have been waiting for years! People with little hope of actually receiving a child anytime soon, given how long the lists of available, approved, adoptive parents are."

"Those families aren't related to William by blood!"

For Thad and William's sake, Michelle wished that was all that counted. Unfortunately it wasn't.

She slowed her pace even more and broke the news to Thad as gently as she could. "Technically, from a legal standpoint, neither are you. Your brother, Russell, terminated his rights at the time he donated the sperm. So legally, he has no say in what happens to this baby. To get those rights reinstated would involve a long, complicated process." A reinstatement that Judge Barnes was, at least at the moment, unlikely to grant.

Thad stopped next to his SUV, the still-sleeping William in his arms. "You said a *private* adoption is possible, if the Johnsons agreed I could have William."

Michelle stepped closer to Thad to allow another couple to pass. "That's right. It is possible. And there *was* a chance," she continued, "had baby William not been dropped off on your doorstep after he was given back to the surrogate, that this petition of yours might have gone through without a hitch. But William *was* left on a doorstep. And it's possible that social services will decide foster care is the way to go for the moment."

Michelle's phone rang. She listened intently to the caller on the end. "Yes," she said firmly, not all that surprised at the speed with which everything was happening now. "He can be there. Fifteen minutes is fine with us."

FIFTEEN MINUTES for what? Thad wondered, studying the concerned look on Michelle's pretty face.

She ended the connection and slid her BlackBerry back into the outside pocket of her briefcase. "Tamara Kelly, the social worker assigned to do the home study and make the evaluation, is on her way to your place."

Thad tried to recall if he had even done the dishes. He didn't think so. In fact, he was certain he'd left his cereal bowl, a couple of baby bottles, as well as assorted cups and glasses in the kitchen sink.

Upstairs, his dirty clothes were scattered across the floor. He hadn't had a chance to fold any of his clean laundry or do anything with the stacks of hand-me-down baby gifts in the living room.

Damn it. If only he'd had some advance notice. Even a half-hour warning would have been a huge help in getting ready for the inspection. But then, he supposed that was the point. They didn't want him to have a chance to do anything that hadn't already been done.

He looked at Michelle. "Tell me you can be there for this."

Michelle glanced at her watch, frowned.

He could see her taking an emotional step back already. She bit her lip. "It's not usually the case to have an attorney present for this."

Thad realized that. He also knew, if Tamara Kelly based her decision on how much laundry had been left undone, or the condition of his bedroom and bath right this minute, there could be a problem.

Normally he did household chores on a semi-regular basis. The past few days, since he'd been taking care of William, he'd let everything—but caring for the baby—go. Whether his bed had been made or his dirty clothes picked up off the floor hadn't mattered. Now, suddenly, they did.

Thad looked Michelle in the eye. "As Judge Barnes pointed out, this isn't a usual case." Thad did not want any more un-expected developments.

Michelle looked at William, then back at Thad. "All right," she said. "Let me call my office and reschedule a few things, and I'll meet you at your house."

By the time Thad got home, a small sedan was already parked in front of it. A tall, efficient-looking woman with frizzy, fading red-gray hair emerged from the car. She smiled at William, who was snoozing away in his car seat, then turned back to Thad and introduced herself as head of the Summit County Child Protective Services Department.

He shook hands with her. "It's an unusual situation," he said.

Tamara Kelly nodded, her eyes kind but impartial. "I un-derstand you're trying to do the right thing," she said gently.

The fortysomething social worker just did not look or sound as if she felt that adopting William was it.

Thad was used to proving himself in his profession—E.R. doctors were constantly put to the test.

Not in his personal life.

Of course, there had never been this much at stake in his private life. Not since he and Sela ended their relationship three years ago.

Another car pulled up. Michelle's. She stepped out, looking calm and professional. She introduced herself to Tamara.

Thad unbuckled William from his car seat and led the way inside.

Tamara Kelly carried a clipboard and pen with her. She looked in every room of the house. Occasionally she asked a few questions. Mostly she just wrote things down. She wrote a lot of things down.

Thad was a confident guy. And with good reason. He had earned everything he had ever gotten. But the silence, the inscrutable expression on Tamara Kelly's face, the fact that she rarely made eye contact with him were making him nervous.

Michelle, for all her outward cool, seemed edgy, too, as they walked past Thad's unmade bed and the borrowed bassinet that now served as William's sleeping berth.

Tad had liked having William close by during the night.

He could see, though, that to the outside observer, he looked completely clueless when it came to setting up for a baby. As if he didn't care enough to do things right.

Finally Tamara made her way back downstairs to the foyer.

Abruptly she seemed more than ready to leave.

Thad looked at Michelle.

Michelle looked at the social worker and said, "We'd like a copy of the report as soon as possible."

"Certainly." Tamara Kelly flashed another officious smile. "I probably won't have it typed up until tomorrow morning."

"Could we have a brief verbal assessment now?" Michelle persisted.

Tamara hesitated.

Thad cut in. "I know the place is a mess. Like most new parents I've been all about the baby for the past few days, but if there's something I need to fix, I'd really like to know about it as soon as possible."

Clipboard pressed to her chest, Tamara took another moment to consider. Finally she said, "Let's sit down, shall we?"

Bypassing the mess in the formal living room, they retreated, instead, to the formal dining room. The table had an inch of dust on it. Ditto the china cabinet. Thad made a mental note to clean those, too.

"Okay, first the things you have going in your favor," Tamara told Thad, her glance touching briefly on the newborn baby sleeping contentedly in his arms. "Baby William has obviously bonded to you. You have a home in a nice, safe neighborhood. A good job and a fine professional reputation, both at the hospital and with our department. There is nothing physically or fiscally wrong to prevent you from becoming a fine parent."

"Great!" Thad said with relief, figuring he'd heard enough to know he'd passed the test.

"And the cons?" Michelle asked, every bit the I-don't-believe-it-until-I-see-it-in-writing attorney.

Tamara frowned. "Your home is not baby-proofed, Dr. Garner. Baby clothes and gear are heaped all over the living room. There's no nursery, no crib set up, no food in the fridge, no spouse or other family member to help with child care."

"I have a babysitter lined up for when I go to work," Thad reminded her.

"And I made note of that." Tamara pointed to her clipboard. "But you've also never been married. Never reared a child. You have a reputation, socially, within the community as a man with a notoriously short attention span when it comes to relationships. The bottom line is you lose interest in a woman after a few dates. How do we know you won't lose interest in a child just as quickly?"

THAD HAD NEVER figured, in his attempt to give every potential woman and relationship a chance to turn into something lasting, that he was making a mistake.

Now he knew better.

And so, apparently, did Michelle Anderson.

He waited until Tamara had left before he turned back to Michelle. "I feel like I'm being unfairly judged here." It irritated him. He was a private person. He didn't "kiss and tell," and he didn't feel—even in this instance—that he should have to explain why he and any woman he had previously dated hadn't been right for each other. It was enough that he and the women knew.

With the exception of Violet Hunter—who still seemed to have a crush on him—all the women he'd dated seemed to agree that they were just not suited for each other.

Michelle shrugged, not at all surprised. "People talk about this stuff—especially in rural communities, where not a lot else goes on."

"But she's a professional."

"Who is doing her job. You don't have a good track record with women here. If, for instance, you had ever been in a serious relationship…"

Figuring if he had to discuss his romantic past with anyone, it might as well be to one of the two lawyers representing him, he looked Michelle in the eye. "I dated a woman for five years, and Sela and I lived together for two after that."

Michelle blinked, stunned. After a moment she pulled herself together and continued in the same tone she probably would have used had she been a prosecuting attorney. "But didn't marry," she said quietly.

A fact, Thad knew, that wouldn't sit well with a stickler like Judge Barnes, either.

Thad went to put the sleeping William in the only available bed nearby—his infant carrier. He knelt to strap him in and tucked a blanket in around him, then walked with Michelle back to the dining room. "Only because Sela wasn't ready."

She stood, hands hooked over the back of the chair where she'd been sitting. "What happened?"

Suspecting Michelle was asking as much for her own curiosity as for the benefit of his case, Thad gestured for her to take a seat again.

When they were settled, he said, "Sela and I met in med school and started dating then. We stayed together until we finished our residencies, both in emergency medicine. Then we were starting to interview for jobs. I would have gone to Houston or Dallas or anywhere else she wanted to be. The big cities were more reasonable because they had a higher likelihood of us both finding positions at hospitals near each other." He paused, remembering the shock and the hurt. "Sela thought it wasn't a good idea, that our relationship had gone as far as it was going to go."

Michelle leaned back in her chair. "And you didn't agree?"

Thad had always wanted to be closer, to have the kind of relationship where they could finish each other's sentences. It hadn't happened. But that didn't mean he and Sela hadn't been happy, spending time together whenever they could. "I expected us to get married and have kids," he said finally.

Still listening, she leaned closer. "And?"

"Sela felt that while we had been a great support system for each other, we didn't have the kind of emotional intimacy necessary to build a future on, have a family. She thought it was better if we called it quits while we were still friends."

Compassion lit Michelle's eyes. "Are you still friends?"

Thad shook his head. "I couldn't go backward in the relationship and that's what it would have been, at least to me. So we ended it and moved on. For a while afterward, I shut down and didn't see anyone. Then I realized that wasn't good, either, so when I took the job in Summit, I decided to put as much effort into finding someone to settle down and have children with as I have everything else." He cleared his throat. "So I've tried to stay open to the possibilities. Not just dismiss women without getting to know them first. The trouble is," he explained patiently, "if you go into the getting-to-know-each-other-phase strictly as friends, you can't get close to each other the same way you would if you were romancing them, but if you're romancing them and it doesn't work out, it can be hard to go back to the possibility of being just friends."

Michelle heaved a commiserating sigh. "Damned if you do and damned if you don't."

"Exactly." As their eyes met and locked, Thad felt a shimmer of tension between them. Man-woman tension. "The thing is," he continued, "I'm not going to give up dating, because I still want to get married and have kids. I want to find that special someone."

And in fact, Thad thought, his spirits lifting, he was beginning to think he already had.

MICHELLE STUDIED Thad, aware once again that the situation had taken an unexpectedly intimate turn. And while, as a woman, as a neighbor, as a friend, she was glad to know that Thad wasn't the player she had thought, as the law partner of his family attorney, it put her in an awkward spot.

"I usually don't talk about my ex," he said.

Forcing herself to get back to business, she reached for the yellow notepad and wrote a memo for Glenn. "It's something the social worker should know." Something *she* had needed to know, too.

Thad grimaced. "Unfortunately Tamara Kelly seems to have formed an opinion of me, and it's the same one you had."

Michelle ignored the intensity of his gaze and kept on writing. "It's hard not to think that with the number of women constantly traipsing to your front door," she remarked casually.

"If you've noticed that, you've also noticed I usually manage to avoid inviting them in."

Playing devil's advocate, Michelle pointed out, "But you often sit on the front porch with them for a while."

"To be polite," Thad qualified, his frustration apparent. "I don't know how to discourage them without hurting their feelings."

Michelle joked, "Rudeness often works. But it'd be a heck of a time to start being rude, when you're trying to adopt a baby."

"Exactly. I need to appear more of a gentleman than ever." Thad met her gaze again. "But if you were interested in me—"

Michelle stopped him before he could go further. "I'm not," she fibbed as her heart kicked against her ribs.

Thad looked at her as if thinking the kiss the other night indicated otherwise. "Let's just pretend, for the sake of argument, you are," he drawled. "What would discourage you from making a play for me?"

That's easy. "If you were involved with someone."

Thad's lips compressed. "I've been dating someone before. That hasn't stopped the female attention aimed my way."

That was because he was such a genuinely nice guy. "It probably would if you were seriously involved with someone."

He ran his palm across his jaw. "You've got a point. I never had this problem when I was with Sela."

"See?" She studied the buttons on his shirt. "Easy."

Thad inclined his head. "Let me get this straight. The judge wants to see me in a lasting relationship. So would the social worker. And you think if I were to see someone seriously, I'd no longer have the problem with all the single women making plays for me. So, in theory, having a steady girlfriend would solve all my problems."

"*In theory* being the key words, Thad. You can't just… I mean you shouldn't…get involved with someone simply as a means to an end." People could get hurt. *She* could get hurt.

He continued to study her as if he was trying to figure something out. "You're right," he concluded. "If and when I do get involved with someone again, it has to be for the right reasons. Because I know even before we have our first date that it's going to work."

"Again that sounds fine in theory, but…"

"Easier said than done," he guessed.

"I think so." Another silence fell. "In the meantime, you have a lot to do." Michelle got up to leave.

"Yeah, I do," Thad agreed.

She packed up her briefcase, then paused to take one last look at the still-sleeping William. "If you need any help…" she murmured, her heart swelling with love for the abandoned baby boy.

Thad lifted his brow. "Are you available tonight?"

Chapter Six

"How did the depositions go?" Michelle asked Glenn. She was about to walk out the door. Her partner was just walking in.

Glenn set his briefcase on his desk. "I think it's going to take several more days before we finish." He removed his suit jacket and looped it over the back of a chair. "How did the hearing go with Judge Barnes?"

Briefly Michelle filled him in, finishing with the social worker's home visit.

"A bad initial report can be hard to overcome," Glenn warned.

But not altogether impossible.

Recalling she had promised Thad she would help out with the baby again that evening, Michelle said, "Between you and me, I don't think Thad considers failure an option in this situation. Which is why I wanted to talk to you. I don't think I should be representing Thad, even in a pinch. Any other one of your clients is fine—I'm happy to help—but I think it's a bad idea for me to get professionally involved with Dr. Garner."

Glenn eyed her with the wisdom of someone who had known her for years. "I thought your days of getting emotionally invested in cases were over," he stated.

So had she, but Thad had a way of drawing her in, making

her feel a part of his—and William's—life. "The thing is, we're neighbors. I don't want there to be any bad blood if things don't go the way Thad wants. It'd be too awkward, living across the street from each other."

"I understand." Glenn paused to peruse the extensive notes she had made for him. "You really think the court might turn down Thad's petition to adopt?"

"I don't know." She only knew she didn't want to lie awake at night worrying about it.

Figuring Thad had probably lined up an army of people to help him get his house quickly up to the standards of children's services, Michelle drove home. She was pleased to see a housecleaning-service van in front of the house. That meant Thad was taking the evaluation process seriously. It would help a lot to have everything sparkling.

She went inside and changed into jeans, sneakers and an old shirt, then walked across the street to see if there was anything else Thad and William needed. Looking incredibly handsome and relaxed, Thad answered the doorbell with William in his arms.

"Are we ever glad to see you!" Taking her by the wrist, he drew her inside the house, past the activity in the living room, dining room and foyer to the kitchen. Overflowing grocery sacks were scattered across the countertops and table. "William and I went shopping," he announced proudly.

His cheerful attitude was infectious. Michelle grinned. "I can see that." Just as she could see what a wonderful dad Thad was going to be.

"We got a lot of different stuff. I was going to put it all away, but the vacuum cleaner startled William and he started fussing, so…would you mind holding him while I heat a bottle of formula for him?"

Their hands and arms brushed as he transferred William to her. To distract herself from the tingling sensation, Michelle cuddled William close and looked around some more. Front and center on the countertop was a very handy gadget. "You got a bottle warmer."

"Yeah, it was in that stuff I got at the shower the other night. I found it when I was trying to sort through it all and put it away. Pretty neat." Thad demonstrated how it worked for her. "You just put a little water in the bottom, set the bottle of formula in the warmer, press this button and then wait for it to heat up."

Michelle smiled. If Thad kept improving his parenting skills at this pace, his next evaluation was bound to be a lot better. There was only one problem. She inclined her head at the groceries. "Are you really going to use all this?"

He looked puzzled. "Why?"

Michelle decided to be blunt. "Because if you don't, and you forget about the fresh produce and the meat and milk, and it ends up going bad in the fridge, that wouldn't look so good, either."

Thad's eyes glittered with undecipherable emotion. "You don't think I can cook?"

Was that a serious question? "Uh…no."

He came close enough for her to inhale the scent of soap and aftershave clinging to his skin. "Why not?" he taunted, looking very much like he wanted to kiss her again.

The damning part was, she wanted to throw caution to the wind and kiss him, too. "You don't have the kitchen of a man who cooks," Michelle said. He hadn't even known what a mixing bowl was.

He gestured toward the cabinets. "I've got pots and pans and dishes."

Michelle did not know what he was used to, but she was not afraid to go toe-to-toe with him. "And as of this afternoon, when Tamara Kelly was here doing her inspection, nothing but juice, coffee, bottled water, formula and milk in the fridge. If you cooked—" she edged closer, further pressing her point "—you would have had eggs and flour and salt and spices, meat and veggies, bread."

He looked at her like he wanted to do a lot more than kiss her. "I had cereal."

She wanted to do a lot more than kiss him, too. "True."

He braced his hands on his waist. "I'm going to learn how to cook."

His nearness had her pulse racing. "Really?"

He nodded. "And I'm hoping you'll volunteer to teach me, starting tonight."

THAD WASN'T SURE what was more disconcerting, the stunned look on Michelle's face as she processed his request or the sight of her standing in his kitchen, cradling William in her arms. Was this what it would be like to be married and have a kid? He'd never felt as close to anyone as he did to the two of them at this moment. And they barely knew each other.

Thad continued casually, "I figure simple is better."

Michelle's pretty green eyes widened. "Don't you think you should slow down?"

"Heck, no." The light on the warmer went off, signaling the bottle was ready. Thad plucked it from the warmer, wiped off the moisture clinging to the bottom, and shook it well. He tested the formula on his wrist. Lukewarm. Perfect.

He waited for Michelle to settle in a chair, perpendicular to the kitchen table, then handed her the bottle. "I know how these things work. Surprise visits always follow the scheduled ones. I'm going to be ready next time. Hopefully with an apron on, looking very domestic."

Michelle snuggled William against her breast. "You're kidding."

Thad watched her slip the nipple into William's mouth. The baby began to drink almost immediately, looking up at her adoringly all the while.

Thad couldn't blame the little fella. He was pretty besotted with her, too.

"I'm kidding about the apron. Not about being ready." He started taking staples out of sacks. He'd purchased everything from canned green beans to dried barley. Salad stuff. Boneless chicken breasts. Fresh fruit. Potatoes. Soups. More cereal. Bread. Butter. Milk. Cheese. A dozen eggs.

"I'm serious about being the best dad ever," he said.

Michelle regarded Thad with new respect. "I'm impressed."

A feeling of accomplishment shot through him. "That's the general idea."

The vacuum cleaner stopped.

The cleaning-crew boss, a middle-aged woman in a uniform shirt and jeans, appeared. "You want to sign here, we'll be out of your way," she said.

"Every week from now on, right?" Thad said.

The crew boss nodded. "Every Tuesday, from three to six."

"See you next week, then."

"Yes. Thanks, Dr. Garner."

The sounds of workers packing up and leaving were followed by the closing of the front door. Thad turned back to Michelle. "Alone at last," he murmured.

"Not quite," Michelle said, looking down at their tiny chaperone.

"So what do you think we should have for our dinner?" Thad asked.

"You're really going to do this? Learn to cook?"

"With your help?" He nodded. "Absolutely."

"Then wait here." She shifted William and his bottle to Thad's arms. "I'll be right back."

Michelle returned a few minutes later with a book entitled *Kids Learn to Cook*. Thad figured the battered volume had to be at least twenty years old. She set it down on the kitchen table, where he could see. "This has everything you need to get started. Seriously—" she grinned when he glanced at it doubtfully "—even a third grader can follow the instructions. I know, because I started cooking with it when I was that old."

"Your parents gave this to you?"

"I wish." Michelle sighed. "No. My gran gave it to me, but she had to keep it at her house. My parents would have *freaked* if they'd seen it."

That sounded bizarre. "How come?" Thad asked. "Didn't your parents want you to learn how to cook?"

Michelle leaned against the kitchen counter. "My father thought it altogether unnecessary. He wanted me putting all my energies toward academic pursuits. My mother thought I should have one or two signature dishes to entertain with, so she brought in a chef to teach me how to make coq au vin and boeuf Bourguignon."

That sounded excessive, too. Thad began patting William gently on the back. "Why French food?"

"Because she taught college French, so it made sense that if I were going to learn to cook something, it would be something she might have taught me."

"Only she didn't."

"Neither of them were really into the whole parenting thing, except when it came to turning me into some sort of child genius." Michelle's lips thinned into a rueful line. "There, they excelled."

"Let me guess. Perfect score on your college entrance exams."

Sadness glimmered in her eyes. "That didn't please them. They were both professors at Rice University and wanted me to go Ivy League all the way. I wanted to stay in Texas and go to college with my friends. And since I had a full ride at University of Texas in Austin, I didn't need them to approve of my decision—or pay for it."

"A rebel."

She nodded self-consciously. "I guess."

"Surely they forgave you for that."

She looked uncertain. "To tell you the truth, I was never all that close to them. I was to others in my life—just not my folks."

His eyes returned to the cookbook with the kid chefs on the front. "Which is where the gran who gave you the cookbook came in," Thad guessed as William burped in his ear.

Smiling, Michelle watched Thad turn William around and offer him the last of his bottle. "I got to stay with my dad's mom whenever my parents traveled on the guest-lecturer circuit—which was practically every summer and during the semester breaks. Gran lived in Killeen, Texas, and was very down-to-earth. She never really understood how her son changed from a humble kid to an elitist snob."

"Is that how you think of him, too?"

Regret flashed in Michelle's face. "Let's put it this way— I didn't have a typical childhood. While all my friends were going out to barbecue places and seeing movies on the weekend, I was attending lectures, going to museums, being tutored in five different languages. We dined out constantly. But only in five-star restaurants. The only time I ever got to go to an amusement park or eat at a fast-food restaurant was when I was on a school field trip." She sighed. "You know how they say kids rebel against whatever their parents want them to be? Well, I craved *normal*. I would've given anything to eat off the children's menu. Since that wasn't possible when I went out with my parents, Gran taught me how to make all the kid-friendly things—which I could only eat at her house. Mac 'n' cheese. Chicken fingers. Grilled cheese."

Thad could only imagine how tough that had been on her. "Did your parents know that?"

"They knew I ate kid-friendly fare when I was with her. I never let on she taught me to cook, though, and such pedestrian fare. I think that might have put an end to our visits."

Obviously the deception had cost Michelle emotionally. "Where's your gran now?" Thad asked.

Sorrow darkened Michelle's eyes. "She died five years ago."

Had Thad not been holding William, he would have taken Michelle in his arms and held her until she felt better. Unfortunately all he could do was tell her how he felt. "I'm sorry."

Michelle accepted his sympathy with a nod. "I had a lot of good years with her. She taught me how to connect with people." Michelle paused, reflecting. "To see more than just someone's career potential or IQ."

"She sounds wonderful," Thad said softly.

"She was." Michelle smiled. "And she gave me this cookbook." She tapped the cover of the much-used instruction manual. "And now I'm lending it to you. So…good luck. Keep it as long as you need it. I know all the recipes by heart, anyway."

MICHELLE SLIPPED out the door before Thad could entice her to stay. She congratulated herself as she crossed the street to her own home. She'd been helpful, neighborly. But she hadn't gotten overly emotionally involved with one of their firm's clients.

Nevertheless, as the evening progressed, she couldn't help

but wonder how Thad was faring. She was still wondering at 6:00 a.m., when she left the house for her run.

Half an hour later, she was back. Thad stepped out onto his front porch before she reached her mailbox, waved her over.

Acutely conscious of the way she must look, in her running shorts and T-shirt, the top section of her chin-length hair caught in a messy ponytail, Michelle sprinted up his sidewalk.

Thad flashed a smile that upped her pulse another notch. "Got something to show you," he announced proudly.

Michelle could have begged off. She had to shower and prepare for work. However, curiosity prompted her to step inside his house. Thad was dressed as casually as she was, in a pair of gray sweatpants and a white T-shirt. William was dozing in a canvas baby carrier strapped to Thad's chest. Something else that was new, which seemed very well suited to his style.

"That cookbook you lent me is great!" he said.

Michelle blinked. "You tried it out already?"

Satisfaction radiated from him. "Sure did. Grilled cheese sandwiches last night. Oven-baked eggs in muffin tins this morning." His grin widened. "I made enough for two."

He ushered her into the kitchen. The table had been set. A bowl of fruit salad and buttered toast sat on the table. The aroma of fresh-brewed coffee and baking eggs filled the air. "I cheated on the fruit salad," he admitted sheepishly. "Got that out of the produce section. But the rest I did."

Michelle checked her watch in amazement. "How long have you been up?"

"Since five. William decided he was done sleeping. I gave him a bottle, but he showed no signs of going back to sleep and fussed every time I put him down. Finally I put him in this—one of the nurses at the hospital recommended it. It works. Little guy goes right to sleep."

Michelle could see why. As she'd thought before, snuggled against Thad's broad chest, who wouldn't want to drift off to dreamland?

A timer went off and he pointed to the oven. "If you wouldn't mind…"

Michelle put the heatproof mitt on her hand and removed the eggs. They looked done to perfection.

Thad pointed. "Those two are yours. There might be a little shell in the other two. It took me a couple of tries to get the hang of breaking the eggs into those little cups." He winked. "Thus, if anyone lives dangerously, it should be me."

Gallant to the core, Michelle thought. She worked the eggs out and slid them onto plates. "The social worker would be impressed if she saw how hard you're working. Although I have to tell you, it's not necessary to do all this. You just have to demonstrate the ability to feed your child. That could be by hiring someone to come in to cook…"

Thad shook his head. "I remember what it was to have our mom cook for us, versus our dad, who never did. Her way left us feeling pampered and loved."

"And your dad's way?"

The expression in Thad's eyes was bleak. "Russell and I felt like a burden to my dad. I'm going to make sure that William knows he is loved."

Michelle couldn't help it. She reached out and touched Thad's hand. "You feel a deep connection to him already, don't you?"

His fingers closed over hers. "It's funny," he confessed. "My whole life I've had trouble feeling as close to people as I'd like—it's as though I can get so close and no closer. But it hasn't been that way with William. From the first moment I held this little guy in my arms, there was something special.

I know it sounds kind of corny…but I know I'm meant to be William's father in the same way that I knew I was meant to be a doctor."

Michelle was impressed. Moved. "You're very determined."

He shrugged. "I'm used to setting goals and getting things done." Thad held out her chair for her. He paused to study her expression. "I can see you still have your doubts, but I'm going to be the perfect father to this baby."

Thad moved around to sit opposite her. "Everything is going to be so well organized and run so smoothly there is no way the court or children's services can say I'm not qualified to be William's dad."

Michelle spread her napkin across her lap. "I admire your determination. I really do. I can see how much you want this."

Thad's glance narrowed. "I hear a *but*," he said.

Michelle instinctively reverted back to lawyer mode again. "But you need to prepare yourself for the fact that despite everything you're doing, Judge Barnes and Tamara Kelly might not see things your way."

Thad didn't speak, and Michelle went on, "I've had unforeseen events develop and seen clients disappointed before. When it comes to child-custody cases, anything can happen. Decisions are sometimes made by the court that don't seem fair."

"Which is why, to do this, I'm going to need someone to stand beside me." Thad leaned toward her. "You've already said you didn't want do to it as my lawyer. Will you stand by me as my friend?"

THAD WAITED while Michelle considered his request.

"I'll be happy to help you, one neighbor to another," she said finally. "But I'd prefer not to get emotionally involved."

Thad dug into his eggs. "You really think my situation is that risky?"

She swallowed and concentrated on her breakfast, too. "It's not that."

"Then what is it?" he demanded.

Michelle looked over at him. "Situations like this heighten the emotions of everyone involved."

Exactly, Thad thought, why he needed a friend and a sounding board more than ever. To see him through it.

"We could become close to each other very quickly," Michelle cautioned.

Thad added salt and pepper to his eggs. "I can see you also have a problem with that."

She grimaced and tore off a small piece of toast. "It wouldn't be genuine intimacy."

"Says who?"

A pulse throbbed in the hollow of her throat, as she admitted in a low, hoarse voice, "Says someone like me, who's been through it and made that mistake before."

Thad wasn't surprised to learn she'd been hurt. He'd known something was responsible for her skittishness where he was concerned. He waited for her to go on. Eventually she did.

"Four years ago I had a client, Jared, whose wife, Margarite, died in childbirth. His in-laws held Jared responsible for Margarite's death because Jared had known about her heart condition when they married. The two of them had agreed they would not have children—too big a risk for Margarite—but she wanted a baby desperately and became pregnant, anyway. They all tried to talk her into terminating the pregnancy, but she wouldn't listen, so Jared did the only thing he could do—he supported his wife." A pensive look crossed Michelle's pretty face. "Unfortunately the doctors were right—it was too much for her, and she died in child-birth. The baby survived. Margarite's parents blamed Jared for their daughter's death, and sued him for custody of their only grandchild."

"That must have been awful for everyone involved," Thad said.

Michelle put down her fork and clenched her hands together. "That's an understatement. It turned into an ugly, pro-tracted battle that went on for almost two years. I not only represented Jared and his son, Jimmy—I fell in love with both of them. The day the court battle ended, with a verdict in Jared's favor, he asked me to marry him. I said yes. But as life returned to normal and the wedding day got closer, Jared realized that although I loved him…he did not love me. Not the way he'd loved Margarite," she reflected sadly. "So we broke up. And I promised myself never again would I put myself in a situation where a man I was attracted to could mistake gratitude for love."

Thad took a moment to savor the fact she had just admitted she was attracted to him. "I can see how that must have been difficult for you," he said after a moment.

Remembered hurt shimmered in her eyes. "Try heartbreak-ing."

"Our situation is different."

She lifted her eyebrows and got up to pour them both more coffee from the carafe. "Is it? You have an adorable baby to whom I'm already feeling emotionally attached. I'm here having breakfast with you, when I should be home getting ready for work."

Thad studied the conflicted look on her face. "This is about the fact I've kissed you and you've kissed me back, isn't it?"

A blush pinkened her cheeks. She stood, restless now. "It's

about the fact I can't stop thinking about the two of you and your situation."

Thad shrugged and, finished with his breakfast, stood, too. "Then we're even, because I can't stop thinking about you, either, in ways that have nothing to do with your expertise in family law or the gentle way you handle William."

Michelle lifted both her hands before he could take her in his arms. "Look, I understand how much is at stake for you here. I wish you all the best. I really do. But beyond that," she claimed, "I can't put myself in that situation again—I'm too vulnerable. And you shouldn't put yourself there, either, Thad. Not under these circumstances."

MICHELLE WORKED LATE the next two days, not getting home until after nine. By then, Thad's car was already in his driveway, the lights on inside. Even at that late hour, there was a steady stream of women driving up and dropping things off—everything from congratulatory balloons to casseroles to festively wrapped gifts.

Often they were invited inside.

More often, they did not stay long.

Michelle figured that was not by the visitors' choice.

After all, who could resist sweet baby William? Or the handsome, eligible bachelor determined to adopt him?

Only her, of course.

Still applauding herself for her practical attitude, she headed to work Friday morning. Stayed unusually late at the office again that evening, not getting home until ten.

Curiously, even though she'd seen Thad leave for work just before eight that morning with William in tow and knew he got off at eight that evening, there was no car in Thad's driveway. No lights on. No sign of either Thad or William.

Michelle told herself she shouldn't be surprised. Friday was a date night, after all.

Thad was single and had made it clear he did not want to go through the adoption process without a supportive woman by his side.

He and William had probably accepted an invitation to dinner at someone's home.

It was none of her business where he was or with whom.

That didn't stop her from wondering—a little jealously, she admitted reluctantly—where Thad and William were as she took a long, luxurious bubble bath and changed into her favorite pair of white satin pajamas.

At midnight, when she finally slipped into bed, there was still no sign of them.

Minutes ticked by. Then half an hour. Another hour.

Michelle was no closer to sleep when finally, at one-thirty in the morning, she heard Thad's car.

Before she could stop herself, she had slipped from bed and moved to the window.

She saw Thad get out of the SUV. Shoulders slumped, he trudged toward the house, unlocked the door and moved slowly inside.

William was not with him.

Or was he…?

Without warning, Michelle recalled news stories of new parents who had become distracted and forgotten they had an infant in the safety seat in the rear of their vehicle.

Surely Thad—an emergency-room physician and determined new father—would not have made a similar mistake, Michelle told herself. A shiver of unease slid down her spine.

But what if he had?

What if William were sleeping soundly in the car?

What if he *wasn't?*

A raft of possible disaster scenarios filling her head, Michelle put on a pair of driving clogs, grabbed her raincoat out of the closet and ran outside.

Shivering in the brisk air, she headed across the street.

Chapter Seven

Thad had just polished off a slice of cold pizza and uncapped a beer when he remembered he'd forgotten to bring in the day's mail. Wearily he went out to the foyer, set his beer down on the table, looked outside, then stopped in astonishment.

Michelle, hands cupped around her eyes, was peering into the back of his SUV.

Curious now himself, he quietly eased the front door open.

She was definitely snooping. Though what she could want with the back of his BMW, was anyone's guess.

"Can I help you with something?" he asked dryly, trying not to notice how good it was to see her again after several days' absence. He was fairly certain she'd been taking great pains to avoid running into him.

Michelle jumped at the sound of his voice.

Just for the hell of it, he reached inside and switched on the porch lights.

Michelle stood there, looking ridiculously beautiful in the glow of soft yellow lamplight and backdrop of dark night sky. Her hair was delectably tousled, her lips soft and bare, her cheeks a becoming pink. She was clad in her raincoat, which fell only to mid-thigh and which was open to reveal a pair of white satin pajamas that elegantly draped her slender form. It was clear, from the imprint of nipple against the silky fabric, that she was cold.

Desire sent an arrow of fire to his groin. Desire, he told himself, he did not want to feel.

"Well?" He arched a brow, waiting. "For someone who eased so deliberately from my life three nights ago, you sure are nosy."

She flushed guiltily. "I'm sorry. I was worried. I was trying to see if by chance you'd accidentally left William in his car seat in the back. But—" she paused and wet her lips "—there's no car seat."

"I leave it with Dotty when I drop him off in the mornings, in case she needs it."

"Oh."

Silence fell between them, more awkward than ever.

Aware she wasn't the only one getting chilled by the brisk mountain air, Thad said, "Anything else you want to know you'll have to find out inside."

Too tired and cold to stand on ceremony, he walked past her to the mailbox, grabbed the few letters and magazines there, then headed back into the house. As he suspected—or was it hoped?—she followed moments later. The first thing he noticed was that she had buttoned—and belted—her raincoat.

She wrung her hands. "I'm really sorry for snooping."

Thad set down the stack of mail. He picked up his beer and took another swallow. It had been a hell of day and appeared not to be over yet. "Are you finished?"

Politeness would have dictated she murmur another apology and leave.

The attorney in her continued with the investigation into what he figured was his overall fitness as a parent. The fact he had done nothing wrong prompted him to make her work like hell for any further information.

"Is William all right?" she asked finally.

Thad turned and headed for the kitchen.

Deciding a second beer wouldn't hurt, he went to the fridge and pulled out two icy bottles. He uncapped both and handed her one.

After a moment's hesitation, she took it.

Eyes on his, she waited.

"Why wouldn't he be?" Thad said.

Michelle sipped her beer. Still holding his gaze, she shrugged. "Because he's not here with you."

"He's still at the sitter's."

"Oh."

Something dark and disapproving glimmered in her green eyes.

Thad scowled, making no effort to hide the fact that he was disappointed—in the way the evening had gone, in her…. "I couldn't pick him up at eight. I didn't know when I would be done at the hospital, so I talked to Dotty and we decided it would be better for all concerned if William spent the night at her home. I'll go get him first thing tomorrow morning, since I'm off tomorrow."

"Oh," Michelle said again, but this time her expression was one of relief.

Obviously, Thad realized, she had jumped to the conclusion that something dire had happened to William.

Sighing, he carried his beer into the living room. She followed him and watched as he sat down on the center cushion of the sofa and worked off his boots. Slouching down until his shoulders were lined up with the back of the sofa, he stretched his legs out in front of him.

Days and nights like this had him wishing he had someone to come home to, someone to unwind with.

Because both club chairs were filled with neat stacks of baby gifts Thad still couldn't figure out where to store, she took the only available other seat, one in the corner of the sofa next to him.

"Must have been some night at the E.R.," she murmured sympathetically.

"Not the kind I ever want to have again, believe me," Thad responded.

"What happened?"

He looked at the way her knee was bent between them. He wished he could go back and erase the whole day for all concerned.

"There was a head-on collision on the highway outside of town. A drunk driver hit a family of six." And that wasn't the worst of it, not by a long shot. "None of them were wearing seat belts."

"Oh, God."

"Both parents and the drunk driver were killed instantly. The children, ranging from one to eight, were all seriously injured."

Her eyes instantly filled with tears, and her compassion reached out somehow to envelop him in a way that words could not. She covered his hand with hers and asked softly, "Are the kids going to make it?"

"I don't know." Thad accepted the comfort of her hand even as he took another long pull on his beer. "We airlifted them to Children's Hospital as soon as we got them stable, but it's not looking good for any of them."

Michelle turned ashen. She tightened her fingers on his and edged closer to him. "I'm so sorry," she choked out.

Thad ran a hand over his face. "If they do make it, at least they've got family in Houston, already on their way to the hospital." Which wasn't, Thad knew, always the case.

Michelle continued staring at Thad. She shook her head, seemingly at a loss as to what to say or do to make things better.

Experience had taught Thad there was no way to do that. "I shouldn't have laid all this on you," he said gruffly. He shook his head, turned away.

"I don't know how you stand it," she blurted. "It breaks my heart when I see a kid that's hurt or sick."

Mine, too, Thad thought.

"You must be exhausted," Michelle said finally.

He was. "That doesn't mean I'll sleep. Too much adrenaline."

Michelle paused, then asked, "How do you usually work it out of your system?"

Thad knew how he wanted to work it off—tonight. He looked at her and said nothing.

She blushed. "Oh."

"Which is why," he told her candidly, wishing he could just haul her into his arms and kiss her, "maybe, you should head on home."

YES, SHE SHOULD, Michelle knew, as they both stood. If she stayed, she would end up in Thad's arms again.

But maybe that wasn't such a bad thing. Just for this one night. Maybe if they made love once, she would be able to get him out of her system. Stop obsessing over his comings and goings, stop thinking of him day and night. Maybe, if they explored the attraction between them, she would be able to walk away. And so could he. Maybe. She hoped so.

"I'm up for it," she said quietly.

He stared at her, as if not sure he'd heard her correctly. "Up for what?"

"You." Her heart racing, Michelle stepped closer. "Me." She wrapped one arm around his neck, threaded the other hand through the hair on the nape of his neck. "This."

Their lips met halfway in a searing connection of heat and need. Wonder swept through Michelle, along with the knowledge that chemistry like this was something to be savored. So what if this pleasure was going to be meaningless and short-lived, she thought, as he swept a hand down her spine, urging her closer. Her breasts were crushed against the hardness of his chest. Lower still, she felt the depth of his need for her.

Thad kissed her like a man who'd been as starved for intimacy as she. He held her as if he never wanted to let her go. And the truth was, she didn't want their passion to end, either. Not without seeing where it led.

Sifting his hands through her hair, he kissed her temple, her cheek, the corner of her mouth. "I want to take you to bed," he said softly.

Feelings ran riot inside her. "Just this one time," she whispered against the encroaching pressure of his mouth.

His eyes darkened with an emotion she couldn't identify, then he was taking her by the hand, leading her up the stairs. They paused on the landing, to kiss, and then again, as they made their way down the hall. When at last they ended up in his bedroom, he slowly untied and unbuttoned her coat, kissing her slowly all the while. She trembled as he took it off. He paused, then moved to turn on the bedside lamp.

She wanted to hurry; Thad wanted to take his time. Kissing her, even as he unbuttoned her pajama top, one button at a time. By the time the fabric fell open, her breasts were aching for his touch. He eased the fabric down her arms, baring her to the waist.

"Incredible," he murmured, rubbing his thumbs across the dusky crowns. He cupped the weight in his palms. "So incredibly beautiful," he whispered.

Through his eyes, she felt beautiful. Sensual. Ready and eager to please. And she wasn't alone.

He guided her backward, toward the bed, bracing her against his arm. Ever so slowly, he lowered her till she was stretched out on her back, then he kissed his way from her lips, to the nape of her neck, the V of her collarbone, the valley between her breasts. She trembled, her arms clinging to his shoulders and neck. She watched, as if in a languid dream, while his free hand explored every curve and hollow of her breasts. Her skin heated. She had never felt this way before. "Thad…" she gasped.

"I know," he murmured. "I'm getting there."

Claiming her lips again, he eased his hand beneath the waistband of her pajama pants. Tenderly caressed her stomach, moved lower… And still he kissed her, over and over, as if this chance would never come again. He knew exactly how to touch and engulf her in pleasure. How not to rush. Silken brushes of his fingertips alternated with soothing strokes of his palm. Almost before she knew it, she was freefalling over the edge. His breath rough against her cheek, he held her until the quaking stopped, then finished undressing her and joined her—naked—between the sheets.

Lost in a world of undeniable pleasure, inundated with the touch, smell and taste of him, Michelle surrendered to the desire flowing through her. Indulging in her most secret fantasy, she took her time exploring his body, too. His skin was warm satin, his muscles hard. Lower still, she found him hot, hard, demanding. Patient enough to wait until she had stroked and loved every inch of him, too, until there was no more holding back. Finally, he was parting her thighs and positioning himself between them.

She trembled as he slid his hands beneath her and lifted her to him. They kissed lingeringly, and then she arched to receive him. The merging of their bodies was as electric as the joining of their lips, the need to explore supplanted by the yearning for satisfaction. Together they reached new heights—until there was nothing but the two of them, this wild yearning, this incredible passion…this sweet moment in time.

THAD HELD MICHELLE close. They'd barely finished, and already he wanted her again. Not just physically, but emotionally, too. And that was definitely worth noting. He wasn't used to being this attached to anyone this soon. Aside from the feelings he had for William—feelings of connection and closeness that had seemed to be there from the very first—he'd never felt as close to anyone as he felt to Michelle in this moment.

And that was something, given they'd barely known each other a week.

He kissed the top of her head, drinking in the orange-blossom fragrance of her hair and skin. Face pressed against his chest, she snuggled against him. "I can't believe we just did that," she murmured.

Thad threaded his hands through her hair, tilted her face up to his. "I can." He looked into the emerald depths of her eyes. "I've been wanting to make love to you since the first time we kissed." He grinned, amending with rueful honesty, "Actually, sooner than that."

Excitement mixed with satisfaction in her husky tone. "When?"

Thad stroked his fingers through her hair. "Even when you wouldn't even give me the time of day." He kissed the smooth curve of her shoulder, the nape of her neck, her high sculpted cheek. "When did you realize you wanted me?"

She kissed his shoulder, the V of his collarbone, the place above his heart. "I don't know."

He wasn't buying the evasion for one second. "Yes, you do," he insisted playfully, stroking a hand down her spine.

She quivered at his touch. Against his bare chest, he could feel her nipples beading. "The first time I saw you mowing the yard."

Aware he was getting hard all over again, he lifted a brow.

She shifted, and he felt the softness of her thighs against the hardness of his. "What can I say?" She shrugged, offhand. "I liked the way you looked pushing a mower."

He laughed. "You're serious."

"Oh, yeah." She smiled dreamily. "You're one attractive guy." She patted the center of his chest with the flat of her hand. "But then you know that." She started to get up.

He caught her wrist and drew her back down beside him. "Not as attractive as you."

She flushed. "I wouldn't bet on that." Her gaze sobered. "Which is why we really need to pull back and think about this."

He rolled onto his side, propping up his head on his palm, draping his thigh over hers.

With her tousled reddish-blond hair, she looked like an angel. "There are times for thinking—" he traced her lower lip with the pad of his thumb "—and times for not." This was, he decided, the latter. He bent to kiss her.

"You're making it very hard to argue," she whispered as their kiss deepened.

Feeling her tremble acquiescently, he kissed his way lazily down her body. "That's because I don't want you to argue," he said.

She sighed as he found her center. "One more time then," she assented, closing her eyes and giving herself over to him. "One…last…time…."

HOURS LATER, Michelle awoke, to find herself cozily ensconced in Thad's strong arms, her head nestled against his chest, her legs draped over one of his. Daylight was filtering in through the closed draperies. She heard a car start up and rumble down the street. With effort, she forced herself to open her eyes. Seven o'clock!

She yawned, extricated herself from the warmth of his limbs and sat up. She shoved the hair from her eyes. "What time were you supposed to pick up William?"

"Seven-thirty." He glanced at the clock and sat up, too.

Michelle rubbed her eyes. "I guess we fell asleep," she said. After the fourth time. Prior to that, they couldn't get enough of each other. Every time she'd even thought about leaving, he'd reached for her. And once she was in his arms, it had been so easy to succumb. To tell herself pleasure was fleeting and she'd had so little of it in her life lately, she deserved at least one night of all-out passion.

Now, in the light of day, she wasn't so certain it had been a good idea. Instead of satisfying her curiosity and getting Thad out of her system, she had only drawn him deeper into her. That couldn't be good for someone trying to maintain a professional distance. And she was trying hard not to get involved with Thad while his petition for adoption was being considered by the court….

Thad kissed the back of her hand and rose. "Want to come with me to pick William up?"

Michelle looked at him in surprise. "Wouldn't that look…"

"Like we were involved on some level? Yeah. Probably."

Thad did not care.

Michelle did.

She didn't want to give anyone, least of all herself or Thad, the wrong impression. "I don't think that's a good idea."

Feeling suddenly shy about her nakedness, she clasped the sheet to her breast. Then she looked at her raincoat and pajamas still scattered on his bedroom floor. She bit down on an oath. "I can't cross the street in that."

He grinned. "Guess you'll have to stay here all day, then."

"Seriously." Michelle dreaded the thought of encountering one of the neighbors wearing only satin pajamas and a raincoat!

"You want me to go over to your place and bring something back for you to wear?"

"That'd probably be worse if someone saw you going in and out."

She couldn't believe it. She was thirty-two years old and about to do the walk of shame.

Thad opened up his closet, rummaged around, emerged with a pair of stretchy, black running shorts and a gray T-shirt. "Put these on, and wear your coat over them, and it'll look like you've been out jogging."

"In someone else's clothes." Michelle ran her hands through her hair. "This is ridiculous."

"My offer to go over to your place still stands."

They heard another car start nearby and drive down the street.

"No." Michelle sighed. "The longer we wait, the more likelihood there is I'll run into one of the neighbors. I'm just going to put on the pajamas and my coat and go home."

"You can always carry a cup of sugar with you. Now that I actually have some in my pantry, you can pretend you came over to borrow some."

"Very funny, doc."

Still not taking this dilemma as seriously as he should, Thad smirked and disappeared into the bathroom.

Michelle used his absence to get out of bed and slip on her pajamas. She ran her fingers through her hair and put on her clogs. She was in the process of picking up her coat from the floor when the doorbell rang.

Michelle turned to Thad, who had just walked out of the bathroom, in the same clothes he'd worn to work the evening before. Morning beard rimmed his jaw. He smelled like mint toothpaste. "Expecting anyone?" she asked, feeling trapped.

Thad shook his head. "Stay here. I'll go see who it is."

Michelle perched on the edge of the bed while he walked downstairs. The doorbell rang again, more insistently this time. When Thad opened the door she cringed when she heard the familiar voice....

THAD STARED at the social worker standing on his doorstep, aware her timing could not have been worse. "I'm here for a second inspection of the premises," Tamara Kelly said briskly.

Not sure what would happen if Michelle were to come downstairs, clad in her pajamas and looking as if she'd just spent the night with him, which of course she had, Thad tried a diversionary tactic instead. "William's not here."

Tamara lifted the glasses on the chain around her neck and peered at him through the lenses. "Where is he?"

"At the sitter's."

"Already?" Tamara glanced at her watch, noting it was seven-twenty.

"He spent the night there. I didn't get out of the E.R. and home until almost one-thirty."

She nodded cryptically.

"I was on my way to pick him up," Thad continued. "So if

you'd like to accompany me, you could check out the place where he stays while I'm at work. I think you may already know his sitter—Dotty Pederson. She used to work in the nursery at the hospital."

"I do. And I probably will pay her a visit at some point, but right now I need to have a look around here."

For the first time Thad lamented the lack of a back staircase in his home. "I probably should go upstairs and tidy up first," he said.

"Actually you shouldn't." Tamara brushed by him, on a mission now. "It's important I see things just as they are."

If it had only been a messy bedroom, Thad wouldn't have cared. But there was no way around the fact that Michelle was up there.

Or not, he thought, as Michelle appeared at the top of the stairs, her jacket buttoned and belted over her white satin pajamas.

"Hello, Tamara," Michelle said pleasantly, descending the stairs as if her presence was nothing out of the ordinary.

Tamara's eyebrows shot skyward.

Whatever she was thinking was definitely not good, Thad noted.

"Counselor. I'm surprised to see you here so early this morning."

"It is early, isn't it?" Michelle smiled and continued coming down the stairs.

Tamara turned to Thad, with disapproval. "Tell me this isn't what it looks like—that you didn't dump the baby at the sitter's so you could…entertain a guest overnight."

Chapter Eight

Michelle knew that making love with Thad—even for one night—would lead to trouble. She just hadn't figured it would be *this* kind of trouble. She took a deep breath. "This wasn't planned," she explained.

"But I'm not sorry it happened," Thad cut in.

Tamara frowned. "Then you acknowledge that the two of you are now…?"

"Involved," Thad confirmed. "And I'm not ashamed of that."

Michelle only wished she could say the same. She hadn't felt this mortified since she'd been caught making out with her first boyfriend when she was fifteen.

"I see." Tamara made a note on her clipboard.

"I'd like this…situation to remain private," Thad said.

Tamara made another note as she walked through the living room, her gaze on the empty beer bottles they hadn't bothered to discard. "You'll have to take that up with your attorney and let him take it up with the court."

Michelle looked at Thad, explaining quietly, "There's no point in fighting this. It'll be in her report. And her full report—not just the selected excerpts she wants him to see—goes to the judge."

"Why?" Thad asked, clearly irked. "What does you being here this morning have to do with my adopting William?"

"It goes toward your fitness as a potential parent," Tamara explained.

"Then I would think it would help," Thad insisted, "for Judge Barnes to know that I am serious about a woman of such fine character."

Tamara's eyes widened.

It was all Michelle could do not to groan out loud. Gently she laid a cautioning hand on Thad's forearm. "I don't think Ms. Kelly needs to know the specifics of our relationship, Thad."

"Well, I do," Thad countered. "I can see what you're thinking, Ms. Kelly, but this is no one-night stand!"

THE MOMENT the social worker left, Michelle turned to Thad. "I want to talk to you." She pushed the words through gritted teeth.

"Good," he said, wanting nothing more at that moment than to rid her of her embarrassment, "because I want to talk to you, too."

"But I want to do it at my house." Michelle lifted a palm impatiently. "I need to get some clothes on."

Thad thought she looked pretty good in her white satin pajamas and trendy little raincoat, but sensed she did not want to hear that. "I still have to pick up William. I should have been there twenty minutes ago."

She nodded, looking almost relieved she would have some time to get over the shock of the social worker's unscheduled visit and pull herself together. "Go ahead and get William. Then come on over."

They parted company. Thad got in his car and drove the short distance to pick up William, who'd just been fed. "He'll probably fall asleep before you get him home," Dotty warned.

Thad smiled. "That's okay. I've gotten the knack of removing the baby carrier from the car seat without disturbing him. He sleeps pretty well in it."

By the time Thad reached Michelle's house fifteen minutes later, William was indeed sound asleep. Thad unlocked the carrier from the base, lifted it out of the car and transferred it and William to Michelle's front porch.

The door opened before he had a chance to knock. She had been waiting for him, it seemed. Hair caught in a ponytail, she was dressed in yellow-and-blue running gear. She looked adorable.

She motioned soundlessly for Thad to put William's carrier on the dining-room table, then turned and moved quietly out of the room and around to the kitchen. She waved Thad into a seat at her kitchen table, where a glass of juice was waiting.

An empty glass sat on the counter. She remained standing. Not a good sign, Thad thought.

"I know you were trying to make the best of a very awkward situation, but you shouldn't have told the social worker that our relationship was serious," she said in the dispassionate lawyerly voice he was beginning to know so well.

Thad rocked back in his chair. He wished she would sit down. "Why not?" he countered, mirroring her faintly contentious tone.

Her green eyes glowered at him. "Because it's not true."

Thad thought about the way they'd made love over and over again. She might want to deny it now, in the light of the day, but in the comfort of his bedroom, she had wanted him every bit as desperately as he had wanted her. "So," he said, "you're saying…?"

Her mouth tightened. "Last night was about sex and loneliness and pure animal attraction."

It had been all that, Thad admitted, but a lot more. And it was time she owned up to that, whether she wanted to or not. He pushed his chair back, stood and closed the distance between them. "I wouldn't have made love to you," he said, "if I hadn't been seriously interested in you, Michelle."

She lowered her gaze. "I know you think that now."

He cupped her shoulders, holding her in front of him, when she would have run. "I'm not your ex. I didn't turn to you out of gratitude."

She shut her eyes against his searching gaze and reminded him in a low, strangled voice, "I know you think that, Thad. I also know that this is a confusing, highly emotional time."

"No argument there," he agreed.

"I know how much you want to adopt William."

Not *want,* Thad corrected silently. "I *am* going to adopt William."

Doubt flashed in her expression. "The court has to agree that it's in William's best interests."

She was sounding like a lawyer again—a worried one. Thad tensed, despite his effort not to let the recent turn of events derail him in any way. "You think they won't?"

"I think the situation is suddenly a lot more complicated than it was," she replied soberly. "And I'm sorry about that. I know better."

Thad could see the emotional wall going up around her heart as surely as if she was erecting it in concrete. He tightened his grip on her shoulders. "I'm not going to apologize to anyone for making love to you last night. Even you."

She extricated herself and turned to face the window over the sink. "You could tell the court it was a mistake, that it won't happen again."

He looked at the lovely line of her back. "Then I'd be lying."

She whirled. "You plan to let this happen again…with William in the house?"

Thad lounged against the opposite counter, hands braced on either side of him. "That's right. But let's stick to the facts, shall we? William *wasn't* in the house last night."

Michelle gestured helplessly. "He easily could have been."

Thad shrugged. Last night had shown him how much he wanted Michelle in his life. Irked at the roadblocks she kept throwing up, Thad stated, "Even if he had been there with us last night, he's way too young to be aware."

"That won't always be the case." Once again, Michelle took on the role of devil's advocate. "And Judge Barnes is old school. He thinks a couple should be married. At the very least deeply committed to each other."

Thad scowled. "Who says I'm not committed?"

MICHELLE HAD KNOWN Thad was going to be difficult. What she hadn't expected was the tumult of her own emotions. She tried again. "I understand Tamara Kelly's poorly timed home visit has backed you into a corner. But we can still turn this around."

"How?" Thad challenged. "By getting married?"

"That's not funny."

He shrugged his broad shoulders affably. "Who's joking? Seriously, if I need to be married in order to adopt, then I'll take that leap. But only," he clarified in a low, husky voice that sent shivers down her spine, "with you."

The notion of the two of them walking down the aisle wasn't nearly as disturbing as it should have been. Michelle drove her hands through her hair. "You're missing the point!" she cried.

Thad crossed to her. "That *is* the point." He wrapped his arms around her, draping her in warmth. "Last night meant the world to me, Michelle. And if you were honest, you would admit it meant everything to you, too."

Before she could do more than take a breath, his lips were on hers, arguing his point, staking his claim, making sure she knew that the chemistry between them was as potent as ever. And as much as Michelle wanted to deny the passion and, more important, deny Thad access to her heart, she couldn't. When he held her like this, when he brought her so close and kissed her so sweetly, so ardently, all her inhibitions melted away. All she wanted was this moment in time, with this man. If William hadn't chosen that exact moment to wake up, fussing, she was pretty sure they would have ended up in bed again.

But their tiny chaperone did sound the alarm. And it was perfect timing, Michelle thought as she showed the two of them the door and then went out herself for an extra-long morning run. She had a lot of thinking to do before she made any more impulsive mistakes. And the rest of the weekend in which to do it.

Like it or not, for the next two days, Thad and William were going to be on their own.

"MICHELLE?" GLENN York appeared in her doorway on Monday morning. "I need to talk to you in my office for a minute, if you wouldn't mind."

Surprised by the grim note in her partner's tone, as well as the request, Michelle rose and walked into Glenn's office.

As soon as she saw who was already there, she knew the reason Glenn had been so cryptic in his request.

Figuring the staff did not need to hear any of what was about to be said, she shut the door behind her. Gave Thad—and the baby in his arms—a brief, assessing glance, then turned back to Glenn.

"What's going on?" she said, knowing it had to be something dire, otherwise Glenn would not have called her in when she had requested not to be involved.

He gestured for her to have a seat in the chair next to Thad. "I had a phone call from the social worker on Thad's case a while ago."

Thad cut in glumly, "Among other things, Tamara Kelly doesn't like the fact I had to leave William overnight with the sitter while I was at work."

"She fears it could be a harbinger of the future," Glenn said. "Given that he's a single parent and has such a demanding job."

Heat moved from Michelle's neck into her face. "Anything else?"

"She wanted to warn us that Judge Barnes is probably going to want to speak to you about your, uh, relationship with Thad." Glenn cleared his throat, looking like he wished he were anywhere but there. "I've already requested the conversation be in chambers, but it's going to be on the record, as will the social worker's written report."

Great, Michelle thought. Well, what had she expected? She'd known, going in, that spending the night with Thad was a mistake.

"As the attorney of record," Glenn continued reluctantly, "I need to know what you're going to say."

The problem was, Michelle thought, she didn't know what she was going to say.

Both men continued to look at her.

Finally, she shrugged. "That it was a…"

"If you say 'mistake,'" Thad interrupted, "I'm done for."

Her law partner put up a cautioning hand. "Not necessarily."

"It'll look like it didn't mean anything, and it did," Thad insisted, not backing down.

Michelle grimaced. She felt like she was sinking. Taking

a deep breath, she tried again. "The thing is, it's private. I don't…discuss that aspect of my life." She met Glenn's eyes. "With anyone."

"As a friend, I understand," Glenn returned. "As Thad's lawyer and a fellow member of the Texas Bar Association, I'm telling you that you don't have that luxury. When Judge Barnes asks you that question—he wants to see the four of us and Tamara Kelly in his chambers at four-thirty this afternoon to discuss the suitability of William remaining in Thad's custody until a decision regarding the adoption petition can be made—you're going to have to be prepared to answer it a lot better than you did just now."

THAD KNEW THAT Michelle did not want William to go into foster care, even for a brief while, any more than he did. He also knew that she'd been steadfastly avoiding him since they'd parted company Saturday morning and wouldn't misrepresent anything she felt to the court.

Unfortunately, before they could discuss the situation further, the clients for her ten-thirty appointment arrived, and she excused herself to meet with the elderly couple.

Glenn looked at Thad. "It'll be fine," the lawyer said.

Thad hoped so.

Judge Barnes's severe expression when they entered his chambers six hours later was not as reassuring.

"Well, seems we've had some developments since this time last week," the conservative jurist said, leaning back in his chair. "For one thing, Dr. Garner isn't the only one who wants to adopt this child."

Thad cuddled William close to his chest.

"I came over Saturday morning to tell you that," Tamara Kelly admitted, "before things took an unexpected turn."

"We'll get to that in a minute," Judge Barnes said gruffly. "Meantime, you should know, Dr. Garner, eleven other families have approached social services and, by extension, this court, and volunteered to adopt William."

Thad couldn't say he was all that surprised.

Word had gotten out. Everyone in the county knew how and why William had been left on Thad's front porch. Hearts had opened up all over the place, which always happened when an abandoned baby made the news. But none of those wanting to help were family.

"They have no blood claim," Thad said. He remembered what Michelle had told him—that from a legal standpoint, in his case, blood didn't matter—but felt he had to play all his cards.

Judge Barnes shrugged. "In your case, Dr. Garner, it's not applicable."

"I beg your pardon, Your Honor, but in this case it is," Thad shot back. "William is my nephew. Initially, yes, it was a shock, finding him the way I did. Even more of a jolt, discovering how he'd come about and been abandoned, first by my brother— who'll never have any idea what he's missing in not raising this child—and then Brice and Beatrix Johnson, who went to such lengths to make his birth happen." His voice cracked. "But I never had any doubt what the right thing to do was, and that was give William a home and the family he deserves."

"Which is exactly what we're talking about," Tamara Kelly inserted gently.

All eyes turned to her. The social worker continued, even more kindly, "No one is saying your heart isn't in the right place, Thad. We all know you want what is best for William."

"And that might be," Judge Barnes intoned, "a mother and father who know what they are getting into and are equipped to care for the child in a more traditional sense."

Glenn broke in. "Judge, the babysitter is a former pediatric and neonatal nurse, who is now retired and has brought up children of her own. William could not be in better hands during the time Dr. Garner works at the hospital."

"That's true," Tamara Kelly said.

So what was the problem? Thad wondered.

Judge Barnes looked at the notes in front of him, then over at Michelle. And Thad knew it was crunch time once again.

MICHELLE HAD THOUGHT she was ready for the inquisition by the notoriously finicky judge. Suddenly everything she had been prepared to say, about her private life being her own and not germain to this case at all, went out the window. She looked over at Thad, at the infant ensconced in his arms, and knew what she had to do—for all their sakes. "I care about William, too, Judge Barnes," she said quietly.

The judge waited for her to go on, one craggy brow raised in silent query.

She knew what he wanted to know, what everyone there wanted to know. "It's true that Thad and I have really gotten acquainted only recently, but there is something between us that is, well, unique."

"Unique," Judge Barnes repeated.

"We're not teenagers." Michelle tried again. "Sometimes, yes, things happen quickly and unexpectedly. You fall in love with someone, a child, or a…a potential mate, and it goes against all logic, and yet…" She glanced at Thad, looking so strong and virile and loving as he held the baby to his chest. "You know if you don't open yourself up to the possibilities being presented and allow yourself to feel these emotions and become involved, that you will always regret it."

"So you're as serious about Dr. Garner as he is about you?" Judge Barnes asked finally.

Michelle locked eyes with Thad.

There was no pressure in his gaze. Instead, she picked up on myriad other sentiments. Interest. Affection. Want. Need. The struggle to understand. She swallowed and looked to the truth deep in her heart. "He and I have found something unique." *Something she had been looking for her entire life and could not walk away from now.* "I plan to see it through and be there for Thad and William…whenever they need me."

Thad's eyes darkened with an emotion that far surpassed gratitude.

She felt connected to him. On the brink of falling for him, head over heels. And he looked as if he felt the same.

Minutes later the session behind closed doors ended.

William was still in Thad's custody.

"Good job in there," Glenn said as he walked Michelle and Thad to their cars.

"We're—Thad—isn't out of the woods yet," Michelle said awkwardly.

Thad shifted William to Michelle's arms while he unlocked and opened the door of his SUV and let some of the sun-warmed air out. She held William close, breathing in his sweet baby scent. Beside her, Thad's expression was solemn.

"Michelle's right," Thad told Glenn with a sigh. "I need to work harder to prove I'm the right parent for him."

Glenn did not disagree.

"What more can you do?" Michelle asked.

Thad shrugged. "I can even the playing field with the other families who want to adopt William."

Michelle's heart began to race. "How are you going to do that?"

"By finding a good mother for him," Thad stated seriously. "A smart, loving woman who would agree to co-adopt William and bring him up with me."

"WERE YOU SERIOUS?" Michelle asked moments later. Glenn had just headed off to his car, leaving Thad and her, still with William in her arms, standing there.

"As a heart attack," Thad said.

Michelle looked into the strong, indomitable lines of Thad's face. "What makes you think Judge Barnes would go for two unmarried people adopting a baby together?"

"He might not. Then again," Thad said, "if the judge's only arguments are that William should grow up with a mother—which is something I happen to agree on, having lost my own mother as a kid—and that I'm having sex outside marriage, then maybe I should just get married and knock off two objections with a single 'I do.'"

Michelle thought it had been wrenching to learn that Jared had confused gratitude with love and asked her to marry him for that reason. But that misstep was nothing compared to knowing that Thad was contemplating marriage for purely practical considerations. Yet she could tell by the expression on Thad's face that his heart was in the right place.

As was hers. There were bigger, more important things at stake here than their own egos. In particular, a child's well-being. "You'd really do that for William?"

"And more. I love him, Michelle. Like my own child. And I know what I said, about him being of my blood, but to be honest, it's not so much that or even the connection I feel with him—the same connection I feel with you—it's the fact that he needs me. He needs you. Look into his eyes. Feel the way he snuggles against you, like you're the only mother he's ever wanted, and tell me you don't feel the same way."

"I admit that…" Oh, what the hell, Michelle thought, swiping a tear from her cheek. "I've loved this child from the very beginning." Working to get a handle on her out-of-control emotions, Michelle swallowed around the tightening of her throat. "But you and I are not in love with each other, Thad."

Thad regarded her steadily. "We could be," he said softly, "given a little more time."

The deeply romantic part of Michelle felt that way, too. Especially given how she'd felt when they'd made love, how happy she was to see him whenever their paths crossed, and most important of all, how often he was in her thoughts these days. And yet…the lawyer in her who'd had years dealing with family-law catastrophes had a much more pragmatic view.

She looked at Thad, as William curled his fist around her little finger and held on tight. "What if what we feel now is as good as it gets? What if we never do fall head over heels for each other?"

Thad shrugged. "What if we don't?" His voice dropped to a soft murmur. "We're sexually compatible. We live in the same town. We both have jobs we enjoy. We both want to be married and have kids and it hasn't happened. Maybe we've been waiting for perfection, and perfection is never going to come along. I, for one, am not getting any younger."

Neither was she.

"William needs us now," he said fervently.

Thad was beginning to make far too much sense. "How do you know another family wouldn't be better?" she asked.

He grimaced. "William's already been rejected and passed off twice. He's settled in with me and he's started to settle in with you, too. Do you really want to see him taken away from us and carted off to a fourth home, in less than—" Thad did the calculation quickly "—two weeks?"

Did she?

MICHELLE THOUGHT about what Thad had said the rest of the evening and all through the night.

By dawn Tuesday morning, she knew what she had to do. Seeing the lights on over at his house, she showered, dressed and walked across the street. Thad answered the door as if he'd been expecting her. "I take it you have an answer," he said.

Michelle nodded. "And the answer is yes." She held up a palm before Thad could interrupt. "But there are some stipulations."

He ushered her inside. "Okay."

Michelle paced his foyer restlessly. "We have to do a trial run."

His eyes narrowed. "In what sense?"

"I want to try out being a mom, the same way you've been trying out being a dad. I want to spend as much time as possible with you and William."

"Judge Barnes is not likely to go for that if we're not married," Thad said.

"And maybe he will," Michelle replied quietly. She was as determined to protect this baby from future heartache and disappointment as she was resolved to shield herself. "If we can demonstrate that together you and I can provide a mother and father's love, a sense of family and all the love William will ever need or want—*without* getting married first."

Chapter Nine

"Michelle's right," Glenn told Thad as the three of them met in Glenn's office a few hours later. William was snuggled in Michelle's arms. "What the two of you are proposing is not without precedent. In fact, it happens all the time. A biological parent abandons the child and/or signs away all rights to avoid being stuck paying child support. And someone else— usually a new girlfriend or boyfriend to the remaining parent—will step in to adopt the child, even if the two of them aren't living together and have no desire to do so."

"And the state allows it?" Thad asked.

"Most judges rule it's in the best interests of the child to have two people legally responsible for the welfare of the child, as long as custody issues are agreed upon and worked out in advance."

Thad's brows lifted. "Custody," he repeated in concern.

Glenn nodded. "You and Michelle are going to have to decide if you want to split the care of William fifty-fifty, with each of you having equal say and equal time with him. Or if you want Thad to have sole custody, and Michelle visitation rights. Then there are monetary issues, as well. To what degree will each of you be fiscally responsible for William's needs?

And most important of all, Michelle is going to have adequate home studies done, so that social services can determine her fitness as a parent."

Which meant, Michelle thought, she would need to have a nursery set up, too.

"What about the relationship part of the arrangement?" Thad asked.

"Don't try to hide anything from the court—or social services," Glenn warned. "Be clear about whatever it is. And be prepared to talk to Judge Barnes about it again during your next court date—a week from Monday."

What if, Michelle thought, *we* don't know what our relationship is?

"Meantime, I'll notify Tamara Kelly that you are petitioning to adopt William, as well, and get her started on your home study," Glenn promised Michelle.

"Thanks, Glenn."

"No problem." Her partner smiled. A devoted family man himself, he clearly wanted this to work out for them the way they wanted.

Yet he was skeptical, too, probably because she and Thad hadn't said they were in love or planned to get married. Michelle had seen it in the brief hesitation in Glenn's actions when they'd first told him why they had asked to meet him at his office.

Michelle, William and Thad left and headed back to Thad's SUV. "I was going to drive to Fort Stockton today to purchase a crib and a changing table. Interested?"

Michelle had already rescheduled her appointments for the next few days. "I'm going to need some baby gear, too." And after that, they could start working out some of the details of their baby-sharing arrangement.

"Wow," Michelle said as they wandered through the furniture store geared exclusively for kids. Thad was carrying William now. "I had no idea they had so many different kinds of cribs and kids' beds."

"Amazing, isn't it?" Thad stopped in front of a wooden crib painted fire-engine red.

Michelle looked at a similar one in white. Then one in mahogany.

She looked back at Thad. "Do you think we should both get the same kind of crib and bedding? Or mix it up a little?"

"Good question." Thad smiled at a red-white-and-blue chenille rug shaped like a dump truck. "The same bedding would make him feel at home wherever he was."

"But it could get a little boring, too."

"I guess different, then," Thad said. "If you don't mind, I'd like to go with the mahogany, and get this car-and-truck sheet set."

"I'll get the white crib, changing table and glider rocker with the animal-safari sheets."

As they went off to find a salesperson, Thad stopped in front of a bed shaped like a boat. He grinned. "Things have sure changed since I was a kid."

Michelle nodded as they passed a very pregnant woman and her husband, along with two toddlers, debating over a train table and easel.

The woman looked up and smiled at Thad and Michelle and the baby in Thad's arms, obviously thinking they were just another family.

The surprising thing was, the three of them *felt* like a family.

"How was your bedroom decorated when you were little?" Michelle studied a vivid display of wall art.

Thad moved in close to make way for a woman with a

double stroller trying to get through the aisle. "It changed. I remember something about a train when I was in kindergarten, and then when I entered elementary school, everyone was really into spaceships. When I outgrew that, my room was more of a mess than anything else. What about you?" He shifted William as they waited their turn at the sales desk.

"I never had a kids' room. My parents believed that traditional little-girl themes—like princesses and kittens—lowered the intellect of the child. So my bedroom was decorated with Renoir and Monet prints, the bed linens were Egyptian cotton. The study desk was really nice, though."

"I bet." His gaze roamed over her silk sweater and slacks. "Were you ever allowed to get dirty and messy? You know, climb trees and ride bikes and all that stuff."

"I was taught how to ride a bike and swim. My mother and father thought those were necessary skills. Beyond that, the only time I was allowed to run free on a playground was at school recess."

"What kind of childhood would you like to see William have?" he asked.

"If I could wish one thing for him, I'd want him to be free," Michelle said. "Free to explore and just be whatever he wants to be." She studied Thad's generous smile. "What about you? What kind of childhood would you like to see William have?"

"I want him to feel loved and wanted, secure in his place in our family and in the world."

They were in the BMW and almost back in Summit when Thad's cell phone rang. The road was treacherous, twisting, with no place to pull over. He inclined his head toward the holder clipped to his belt. "Would you mind grabbing that and just hitting the speaker button? I'll take it from there."

Flushing a little, Michelle did as directed.

"Thad Garner," he said.

"Hey, Thad. It's Violet Hunter. I just saw your message. And I think I might be able to help you out."

Thad kept his eyes on the road. "Actually, Violet, it's not a good time to talk. I'm driving back from Fort Stockton. I'll get back to you later," he said.

"I'll wait for you to call," Violet said cheerfully.

Thad hit the off button. As the road straightened out, he shifted and slid the phone back in his belt clip.

Michelle knew that whatever Thad wanted to talk to Violet about was none of her business. It shouldn't even matter that Violet still had a crush on Thad. Still, it bothered her. By the time they reached Summit, Michelle knew what she had to do. She turned to Thad as they got out of the car.

"If you wouldn't mind, I'd like to have William by myself for a while this afternoon. See what it's like to be a mom, instead of just a family friend."

Thad thought for a moment, then said, "Good idea. I've got some work to do on the nursery at my house. It'll go a lot faster if William is with you."

HOLDING WILLIAM in her arms, Michelle walked through the house and tried to see the place as a social worker would.

Her home was definitely the abode of a single woman. The downstairs living room had cream-colored furniture, elegant lamps and beautiful framed prints on the walls. The television was hidden in a stylish armoire. Even the coffee table was an elaborate creation of glass and wood. There wasn't a toy or piece of baby gear in sight.

The dining room was formal, the kitchen outfitted with every gourmet-cooking appliance imaginable.

The second floor of her cozy Arts and Crafts house was

just as elegant—and the reason she'd bought the house. The previous owner had raised the ceiling to the attic rafters, ripped out the second bedroom and turned it into a sumptuous master bath with a huge, built-in closet. There was no place for a nursery on either floor.

But there was plenty of room in her heart, Michelle thought as she carried William back downstairs and settled with him on the sofa. If only she hadn't fallen in love with a child before, to disastrous result, she thought, resting her cheek against the downy softness of William's head. Maybe then she would feel a little more confident that it was all going to work out. That Judge Barnes would see she was the mother this little boy wanted and needed.

As an attorney, she knew it was up to her to make sure he did. Feeling empowered, now that she knew what she had to do, Michelle headed back across the street.

Thad answered the door. He was dressed to work—in an old T-shirt, jeans and sneakers. He had a smudge of navy paint across his jaw, another across his cheek. Perspiration clung to his forehead and the back of his neck. He looked at the baby dozing in her arms. "Everything okay?"

"We need to talk," Michelle said.

HE NOTICED William was swaddled. "I forgot to give you something for William to sleep in, didn't I?" he said.

"It's okay. I forgot, too." Michelle was already heading for the Moses basket in the corner. She gently lowered William into it. He stirred, as if trying to wake up. Spreading her palm across the width of his chest, she touched him lightly, all the while shushing him softly.

After a moment he seemed to settle. Then he was asleep. Michelle backed away quietly.

Figuring he might as well get her opinion on something while she was here and happy to postpone whatever it was she needed to tell him, Thad motioned her up the stairs. "Where'd you learn to soothe him like that?" he whispered, impressed she'd managed to keep the baby from waking up during the transfer from arms to bed.

Michelle shrugged. "I figured it out on my own. He sleeps best when reassured—by touch—that he's not alone."

Or been abandoned again.

"That's why the canvas baby carriers work so well."

"Ah." Thad led Michelle into the room that had once been his office. And was now—thanks to some marathon clearing out and transferring to the garage—soon to be William's nursery.

"I went to the paint store and got this child-safe, fume-free color, but once I started to put it on…" Thad looked at the wall he'd painted. "What do you think? It's too dark a blue, isn't it?"

Hands on her hips, Michelle stepped back and regarded what he had done. "To do the whole room in? Yeah, it is." She tilted her head to one side. "Unless you want it to always feel like nighttime in here."

Thad sighed in frustration. The color was good for sleeping, not playing. "Not exactly the look I was going for."

Michelle tossed him a reassuring smile. "All isn't lost. You could use it on the lower third of the wall and then paint a lighter blue above that. I'm sure William would like that."

Thad exhaled in relief. He was trying to be superdad here, but decorating really was not his thing. "I want to get this done today, so I can at least get his crib up before the next unannounced visit from Tamara."

"Just make sure you get the same undertone in each shade," Michelle cautioned.

Thad blinked. "Say that again?"

Michelle checked her watch. "Tell you what," she said, making note of the color shade written on the can. "I'll run to the paint store now. Anything else you need?"

Thad shrugged. He hadn't a clue. "You tell me."

Michelle looked around again, seeming to miss nothing, regarding his amateurish attempt. "I'll be right back. And, Thad, I know the manufacturer said no fumes…"

Thad knew where she was going with this. Before, it had been just him. Now, William was in the house, too. "I'll open all the windows on this floor," he promised.

Thad kept an ear out for William as he measured the wall into thirds and penciled in a line. He even went down and checked on William once he'd taped off the areas to be painted. To his amazement, the little guy kept right on sleeping.

There was a click behind Thad as Michelle let herself in the front door.

She had changed into an old T-shirt, sneakers and a pair of worn, paint-splattered jeans. She set down the paint can she'd bought and tiptoed over to where he stood. "Guess we wore him out with our shopping trip," Thad whispered.

Michelle nodded and leaned in for a closer look. "There was a lot to look at," she whispered.

He followed her back to the foyer, picked up the five-gallon can and sack of supplies she'd purchased. They headed up the stairs.

She knelt to pry open the can. Thad took a look at the co-ordinating pale blue shade. "That's nice."

She'd also bought an extra pan and roller.

"How about you take the top and I'll take the bottom? Since you're tall and I'm not."

"No problem." Their fingers touched as he handed over the

roller, already saturated with the dark blue paint. Relishing how good it felt to be working side by side with her on this, Thad asked, "So what did you want to talk to me about earlier?"

Without warning, she seemed to be holding him at arm's length once again. "I was thinking we should sit down as soon as possible and work out our custody arrangement." She sounded practical, matter-of-fact. "You know—what nights I'll have William, when you'll have him…and then we'll draw up a plan."

"Alternate holidays," Thad joked, thinking how much this sounded like they were splitting up, instead of coming together.

Michelle tensed. "Yes," she said slowly, concentrating on her painting now, "I suppose that, too."

That wasn't what Thad wanted. He had no qualms about making his opinion known. "Do we really have to be this regimented about it?" he asked. He had envisioned a much looser arrangement. One that had them popping in and out of each other's homes, at whim.

Michelle painted the same way she made love, with slow, thoughtful strokes. "The court will want to know, Thad." She focused on her task. "And I think it's best. This way we'll avoid any misunderstandings."

"Like what?" Thad countered, feeling as if they were on the verge of their first fight.

Finished with the spot she was in, Michelle shifted several feet to the left. "We should split the cost of William's babysitter. Whoever is off first should pick him up."

Thad used a brush to paint along the trim line. "That seems reasonable."

Michelle pressed her lips together. "That way he won't have to be with the sitter more than three or four days a week at most. As for nights…that's a little trickier. I'd like to have him fifty percent of the time, if that's okay with you."

Wow. She *had* thought this out. Though Thad knew it was only fair she enjoy her share of nighttime feedings, since those were the times when William was likely to be most in need of rocking and cuddling.

"What else?" He tried not to think about the evenings he wouldn't spend looking after William anymore. Funny how quickly the little guy had become a major part of his existence, to the point Thad could no longer imagine his life without him.

"My home," she said, "is not set up for a separate nursery. I can put the crib and changing table in my bedroom for now, but eventually, I'm going to have to hire an architect and put a two-story addition on if I want a room for William upstairs next to mine. Which I do."

"Okay," Thad said, not sure what she was getting at.

"And it could take a while to get the construction completed. In the meantime, I really think he needs the comfort and stability of his own nursery."

His hopes for a more congenial arrangement rose. "You want to stay with us on the nights you're the responsible parent?" He could go for that.

She looked at him as if shocked he would think her so presumptuous. "I want us to do what some divorcing couples do when they share custody and want to give the kids the reassuring comfort of their own space, in their own home. It's called 'bird-nesting.' The kids stay in the same place—it's the parents who come in and out, when it's their turn."

"So on your nights, you'd sleep here…"

Michelle nodded. "And you'd sleep at my house, in my bed."

Thad could easily imagine trekking everything back and forth, but to sleep in her bed—and have her in his? How would he be able to do that and not think about making love to her again?

But then, maybe that was what this was all leading up to. Maybe she just needed him to slow down in the romance department while they figured out how to co-parent. All Thad knew for certain was that he wanted to be with Michelle as much as he wanted to be with William.

A spot of color appeared in Michelle's cheeks. "It would certainly keep us from having to duplicate everything—in the short term. Until the adoption goes through, officially. And then, as William settles in and I get a place set up for him in my home, we could gradually transition him into spending half his time with me and half his time with you."

"Sounds…complicated," Thad said. Almost as if she already had one foot in the door and one foot out.

"Not really," Michelle said, not meeting his eyes. "This is actually going to be easier for us in the short term. And it's not like William would never be at my place with me. He would be. At first, like now, for small periods of time. For afternoons. Naps. While I'm also doing laundry and things like that. But once the construction starts, you know as well as I do that it'll be too noisy and disruptive for him to be there."

She had a point there. The sound of nail guns and hammers drove him crazy, Thad thought, and he was an adult. Just the sound of the vacuum cleaner had awakened and frightened the little guy the other day.

Michelle knelt to refill her paint tray. "The bottom line is, we have to be as proactive and consistent as possible in what we do where he is concerned."

"And here I thought we'd just parent by the seat of our pants," Thad joked.

Michelle lifted a censuring brow and rolled the last of the dark blue paint on the lower walls.

Thad had seen women lose their sense of humor when it came to issues like this. He'd hoped Michelle would not be one of them. He cleared his throat. "Seriously, I see your point. Although I don't think William is all that aware of his surroundings."

"But he will be," Michelle predicted. "He's getting more and more alert every day."

"Speaking of which…" Thad finished applying the light blue paint and set the roller in the tray. He glanced at his watch. It had been nearly four and a half hours since the last feeding. "William should have been awake half an hour ago."

Alarm flashed in Michelle's eyes. Thad knew exactly how she felt. Usually William let them know when it was time to feed him.

"I'll check on him." Michelle was out the door like a shot.

Thad was hard on her heels.

They bounded down the stairs and into the living room, over to the Moses basket, where William was sleeping.

Eyes open, he had worked one arm out of his blanket and was lying quietly, looking up at the ceiling. Although he wasn't making a sound, Thad noted his cheeks looked a little pink.

"Hey there, little fella," Michelle said, reaching down to pick him up.

She frowned as she held William. "Thad? I think he feels a little warm."

Chapter Ten

"Thanks for meeting us at your office," Thad told his colleague Sandra Carson forty-five minutes later.

"No problem." Sandra switched on lights as she went. The forty-two-year-old pediatrician was dressed in jeans and a T-shirt bearing the name of her youngest daughter's T-ball team. "The game was just over when you called and the kids were going out for pizza with their teammates. My husband will bring them home." She winked. "As well as a little dinner for me." Sandra paused to wash her hands at the sink, then looped her stethoscope around her neck. "So what's going on?"

"William woke from his nap with an elevated temperature." Thad laid William on the examining table. The baby began to cry. Beside him, Michelle looked about to tear up, too. Realizing for the first time what it was to be the *parent* of a kid in this situation, instead of the doc in charge, Thad swallowed around the unaccustomed lump of emotion in his throat. "I know what I think it is, obviously, but I wanted an expert opinion."

"Well, you've come to the right place." Sandra unsnapped the knit sleeper. Her expression intent, she listened to William's heart and lungs, then gently palpated his abdomen, checked him for any stiffness, looked into his throat, ears, nose. "There's an enterovirus going around—usually lasts around three days—but I want to do a little blood work to confirm."

Thad had expected as much. He began to relax. "We've been seeing it in the E.R., too."

"It's that time of year," Sandra said sympathetically. "My kids had it week before last. They weren't feeling very well, but they were happy to miss school."

Michelle and Thad both chuckled.

"If you'll hold him, I'll do the prick," Sandra said.

Michelle winced as William let out an enraged wail. Empathetic tears slid down her face.

"I'd like to get his temp again, too, when he calms down," Sandra said before slipping out of the room.

Not sure who needed comforting more, Thad handed William to Michelle. The moment the little guy was wrapped in her arms, he stopped crying. "Guess he knows who his pals are," Thad said.

He reached for the thermometer. While Michelle continued to hold William, Thad took his temp again, as unobtrusively as possible. By the time Sandra came back in, the thermometer had beeped. Thad read the results out loud. It was a degree and a half above normal.

Sandra made note of it on William's chart. "Not too awfully high, but you'll need to keep an eye on it." She looked up. "The blood test showed it's not bacterial. So the treatment, as you know, is going to be acetaminophen, fluids and a lot of TLC. He may get a little worse before he gets better. Most important thing is to keep him comfortable, well-hydrated and his temp down." Finished, Sandra held out her hand to Michelle. "I'm sorry. We got down to business so fast, you and I haven't been properly introduced. I'm Sandra Carson, William's pediatrician. And you are…?"

"Michelle Anderson, Thad's neighbor…"

"And William's mom," Thad finished.

THAD'S COLLEAGUE looked like she could have been knocked over with a feather, Michelle thought.

"We're both petitioning to adopt him," she explained.

Sandra looked at Thad. "I didn't even know you were involved with anyone."

"He's not. I mean, we're not," Michelle said, aware that even as she spoke the words felt untrue. Because they *were* involved, more so with every moment they spent together. Just not the way people expected.

"It's complicated," Thad said.

Michelle pretended an ease she didn't feel. "A friends-becoming-family thing."

"Michelle will be every bit as involved in William's care as I will be," Thad stated casually.

Sandra blinked. "That's great. Congratulations. William is one very lucky boy."

"You okay?" Thad asked, when they were back home and getting William out of the back of his SUV.

Michelle nodded, though in truth she still felt a little shaky. It was always upsetting when a little one was sick. And with William barely two weeks old… She swallowed. "I know it's supposed to be my night to take care of him, but I'm thinking…under the circumstances…that we should do it together at my house."

Noting William had drifted off to sleep again on the short drive home, Thad left the baby strapped in the car seat and lifted the infant carrier out of the base. "Agreed."

Trying not to think how nice it would feel to be with Thad all the time, Michelle walked slowly toward his front door. "One of us will have to sleep on the sofa bed."

A warm spring breeze drifted over them. "No problem," Thad said.

She studied the gentle, respectful light his eyes. He had such an easygoing attitude. "You sure?"

Thad nodded. "With him sick, I wouldn't be comfortable away from him. And as William readily demonstrated in Sandra's office, he needs you, too. So what do you say we gather up everything we need and then head across the street?"

Relieved they were on the same page, Michelle said, "Sounds great."

They walked into the house. Michelle noted that the red light on Thad's phone in the foyer was blinking. "Looks like you've got a message."

Thad set the baby carrier down on the living-room floor, well out of any draft and away from any noise. He came back and punched the play button. A female voice floated out from the machine. "Hey, Thad, it's Violet. How come you haven't called me back? I thought you really needed my help ASAP but—"

Thad punched the end button. "I'll listen to the rest of that later." Guilt flashed across his handsome face as he studied her stricken look. "I know what you're thinking. It's not what it sounds."

That was good, Michelle thought grimly, because it sounded like he was two-timing her—or would have been, had they been dating. Which, Michelle reminded herself firmly, they were most definitely not.

"It doesn't matter," she said.

"It does." Thad caught her by the shoulders and turned her to face him.

Michelle held on to her dignity by a thread. Aware she'd already inadvertently revealed far too much of her feelings, she said as nonchalantly as possible, "Look, you're free to date whoever you please, whenever you please. I am, too."

He let her go. Stepped back. Studied her face, his own expression impassive. "That's really the way you want it?" he asked. She noticed that his voice was a bit hoarse.

She avoided his gaze. "We're both adults, with needs and…and desires. Simply put, this is the only way this arrangement of ours is going to work."

MICHELLE'S VIEW on how their parental partnership should be conducted did not change Thad's mind about where he wanted their relationship to go. But figuring his agenda could wait until after William was well, Thad did not pursue the issue. Rather, he said simply, "No matter what, Michelle, I want us to be friends."

"I do, too."

"Good. So, on to getting what we need for the evening ahead…"

While William continued to sleep in the baby carrier, Michelle collected clothing, blankets and diapers. Thad got the bottles, formula, baby first-aid kit containing acetaminophen and his medical bag. They heaped everything into an oversize laundry basket and took William across the street to her house.

Since the things they had purchased would not be delivered until later in the week, Thad returned for the portable crib and Moses basket. Realizing belatedly they probably needed the baby bathtub and assorted baby lotions, cleansers and wipes, he returned to get those, too.

When he came in, Michelle was in the kitchen, a fussing

William in her arms. A half-made bottle of formula sat on the counter. "Need a hand?" Thad asked.

She nodded, her relief palpable. "I don't know how single parents do it."

Neither did Thad. He needed Michelle tonight, as much as William did.

Quickly he finished preparing the bottle and handed it to her. Michelle leaned against the counter and gave William the bottle. He drank a small amount, then started to drift off to sleep.

Michelle looked at Thad, a question in her eyes.

"We have to get more fluids than that into him," Thad said.

Michelle shifted William to her shoulder, jostling him enough to wake him. She patted him on his back. He looked around, seeming listless and out of sorts. "I feel so bad for him," she murmured.

"He'll get through it," Thad promised.

When William burped, Michelle tried again.

William sucked on the bottle without much interest. It took quadruple the amount of normal coaxing to get two ounces into him. Finally he pushed the nipple out of his mouth.

Thad touched the back of his hand to the little guy's cheek. It was cool. The acetaminophen they had given William in Sandra's office was doing its job. "Maybe we should put him down for a while and try again in two hours, instead of the usual four," Thad suggested, knowing they were likely to have a long night ahead.

"SURE YOU HAVE everything?" Michelle asked Thad some five hours later. Thad looked at the sofa bed she'd made up for him in the living room. It was outfitted with cream-colored sheets, the same hue as the sofa, and a matching quilt. The pillows looked luxurious.

William was already settled in the mesh-sided portable crib upstairs next to her bed. Pushing aside the yearning to take her in his arms and give her a proper kiss good-night, Thad said gruffly, "I'll be fine. Let me know if you need me."

"I will." Looking for a moment as if she wished he would kiss her, she gave him one last, grateful glance. "And thanks for staying over."

"Nowhere I'd rather be," Thad said.

Michelle smiled and slipped upstairs. Thad heard her moving around on the second floor as he went into the guest bath to change into a clean T-shirt and jersey sleep pants. By the time he'd climbed beneath the sheets, all was quiet again. He turned off the light and lay there, thinking about the day they'd had and the many more ahead of them. The next thing he knew Michelle was standing next to the sofa bed.

"There's something wrong with William, Thad!" She shook him roughly. "Come quick!"

He leaped from the sofa bed and raced up the stairs after her.

William was still in the portable crib. He was lying on his back, trembling and uttering a weak, distressed cry. Thad didn't even have to touch him to know he was burning up. Calmly he lifted William and carried him over to the rumpled covers of Michelle's bed. Although his adrenaline was pumping, his actions were measured as he coated the rectal thermometer with petroleum jelly. "Fill the baby bath with lukewarm water. Get a towel ready, and a clean diaper and change of clothes. I'll be right in."

By the time he entered the bathroom with a naked, still-whimpering William, Michelle was ready for him.

Thad eased the baby into the tub, holding his tiny body in the palms of his hands. Being careful to keep the little guy's face and neck above water, Thad said, "We need to lower his temperature as quickly as possible."

Michelle edged in, her expression one of maternal distress. "How can I help?"

"Sponge him down with that washcloth."

Michelle gently did as directed. "How high is his temp?"

Thad noted she was shivering, too. Probably from anxiety, since the interior of the house was warm and draft free. "One hundred three point eight—almost three degrees above normal."

"When do we worry?"

"If it goes any higher, but it won't. I just gave him another dose of acetaminophen. That, plus the bath will help."

William's wailing approached a normal pitch.

Over and over, Michelle gently sponged him down. "He really doesn't like this," she murmured to Thad.

"I know," Thad said, cradling the infant in his hands. "But he'll feel better soon, I promise."

Together they worked on cooling William's fevered skin, both of them reassuring him with touch and soft words. William continued to cry. Finally Michelle began to sing. She had a lovely voice, clear and lilting. As the sweet sound filled the bath, William's cries lessened, then eventually stopped. As his body temperature fell to normal, he looked up at Michelle, with a mixture of wonder and what Thad could only describe as love. And the most incredible thing of all was that Thad felt it, too.

IT WAS ONLY LATER, after they'd diapered, dressed and fed William half a bottle of formula once again, that Michelle realized the front of her satin nightshirt was all wet. For modesty's sake, she'd left her bra on. It wasn't doing much to hide the shape of her breasts.

Blushing, she turned away as Thad settled William in his crib once again.

William's eyes blinked sleepily, then finally closed.

Thad stayed there, hand spread lightly across William's chest, waiting until their baby's breath was deep and even.

Slowly he straightened.

He and Michelle looked at each other, as wide-awake and filled with adrenaline as if they'd just started a 10K race.

When she went into the bathroom to clean up, she shivered. By the time she'd dumped the contents of the baby bathtub and set it in the shower to drain, Thad was behind her.

"Sorry if I kind of ordered you around," he said after a moment.

That wasn't why she was upset. "Are you kidding?" Aware she was trembling all over, she released a nervous breath. "I would have been beside myself had you not been here." She paused, dropped her gaze, nibbling anxiously on her lower lip.

Then, on impulse, she looked up into his eyes and confessed. "Oh, who am I kidding? I *panicked,* Thad. I saw William like that and I knew he was sick and…all I could think was I had to get you as soon as possible."

Thad leaned on the edge of her bathroom sink. "That makes sense. I'm a doctor."

She threw up her hands in frustration. Helpless tears stung her eyes. "But if I'm going to be his mother, I should know what to do!"

"And next time," Thad countered implacably, "you will."

Michelle was not so certain. She shut her eyes. Another shiver went through her. The next thing she knew Thad's arms were around her waist. He stood and pulled her into the strong, reassuring cradle of his arms. "It's okay," he whispered, his breath warm and tender against her ear. "I was scared, too."

Michelle sniffed. "You couldn't have been."

"Oh, yes, I could've." He tucked a hand beneath her chin, lifted her face to his. "I see much worse in the E.R.—but none of those patients are my own kid. I have to tell you, what happened just now, the way I felt…the way we *both* reacted, gives me new insight into the way parents of patients behave. It *is* scary when your kid is sick. I don't care what kind of medical expertise you have. The feeling of helplessness—our inability to keep this from happening—is overwhelming."

Thad's confession prompted an admission from her. "I love him, Thad," she whispered, her voice thick with tears. "I know we haven't had him all that long, but I love him so much."

"I love him, too," Thad said.

"If anything were to happen to him…" Her voice broke. She began to cry in earnest.

"I know," Thad said in a low, choked voice. He stroked her hair. "I know."

Michelle tilted her face up to his, needing the reassurance of his gaze as much as she needed his warm, strong arms around her. Thad stared into her eyes and tilted his head. The next thing she knew his lips were connecting with hers, his kiss brimming with all the compassion, comfort and security she needed.

Michelle hadn't expected to make love with Thad again. She'd told herself she wouldn't fall victim to such impossible yearning again. But suddenly she needed to draw on his strength. She knew they weren't in love, but when she was with him like this, she felt loved. She felt secure in this moment, in her life, in a way she never had before.

Thad let her be who she was, gave her the space she needed, and his acceptance made the years of crushing expectations and narrow parameters of behavior fall away. When she was with him, she was free to go after what she wanted, free to express herself in any way she pleased. And what she wanted tonight, she thought, as his hands found her breasts and their kiss deepened, was Thad.

Thad knew Michelle was overwrought. He was, too. It was hard as hell seeing their son sick. The doctor in him knew William was going to be okay in another day. That didn't make it any easier to see their baby boy run a fever so high he trembled, was robbed of his appetite. It broke Thad's heart seeing William so miserable. And it was just as hard seeing Michelle upset, knowing that despite the temporary reprieve that had William fever-free and blissfully asleep, they had another twenty-four hours to go.

Instinct had him seeking comfort in her arms, the same way she was seeking comfort in his. The need to make her his had him unbuttoning her nightshirt, slipping his palms inside.

And once he felt her surrender, felt her body molding to his, there was no stopping with just one kiss. Her nipples budded against his palms. Her silky flesh warmed. He stroked, he kneaded, he caressed, until she surged against him, threading her hands through his hair, kissing him back eagerly, tongues melding in pleasure. Needing more of her, he slipped his hand beneath the hem of her nightshirt, smoothing his palm across her thighs.

She moaned at the new, deeper intimacy and shifted her hips, moving back slightly, giving him access. Throbbing with the need to possess her, he eased a hand beneath the elastic of her panties and found her to be just as soft and womanly as he recalled.

"Don't stop," she murmured, arching against his touch.

Thad groaned as she found him with her hands, too. "I don't intend to." He stepped free of his sleep pants at the same time she kicked off her panties. Moments later, he lifted her up onto the bathroom counter. Need pouring through him, he stepped between her spread thighs. Still kissing him ardently, she hooked her legs around his waist. The intoxication accelerated. And then there was only the touch and taste and smell of each other, the feel of their hands stroking as they gave and received, over and over. She was coming apart in his hands. With a soft moan of wonder, she whispered his name, then, "Now."

"Now," Thad agreed.

Hands beneath her buttocks, he pulled her to the edge of the marble counter, lifted her slightly and ever so slowly entered her, became a part of her. She shuddered and wrapped herself tightly around him. "Thad," she whispered again, still kissing him ardently, making him feel, want and need in a way he never had before.

Their mouths and tongues began to play the same age-old rhythm as their bodies. She gave him everything, demanding more. Sensation built on sensation, pleasure on pleasure, conjuring up passion and surrender, until all control ended, and together, they soared into white-hot oblivion. Stayed, suspended there…and then floated slowly back to reality.

MICHELLE HAD NEVER felt anything like this before. Never wanted anyone as intensely as she wanted Thad. And suddenly she knew it didn't matter how many times they made love, she was always going to want him in her life in exactly this way. And that scared her more than she was willing to admit.

She had given her heart away before, to disastrous result. She did not want to make the same mistake twice. Nor did she want to walk away. The thought of never making love with

Thad again was impossible to bear. Which left her, she admitted ruefully, in a quandary.

How could she continue to make love with Thad, spend time with him and not fall head over heels in love with him?

His body still a part of hers, Thad cupped her cheek in his hand. "We don't have to figure it all out tonight," he said quietly.

A small gasp escaped her lips.

Leave it to Thad not only to see the private worry she would rather have kept hidden, but address it. "You're right." She forced herself to be practical, too. "Our primary objective tonight is taking care of William."

His eyes darkened at the off-putting sound of her low tone. Something in his gaze shifted, grew less intimate, too, even as he made no move to disengage their bodies.

"And to that end…" Michelle continued, but now there was a telltale rasp in her throat. She trembled at the realization of the resurgence—not dwindling—of Thad's desire, the rekindling of her own. "We, uh, should figure out how we're going to do this."

Thad flashed the grin of an unrepentant sinner. "I'll tell you how we're going to do this." He lifted her against him—her legs were still wrapped around his waist—and he leaned down to whisper in her ear. "We're both going to sleep upstairs in your bed tonight."

Her breath caught halfway up her windpipe. She hadn't known it was possible to be so thrilled and reassured both at once.

"We're going to check on William, and make sure he's still all right, and make love again. And then," Thad whispered, "we're going to go to sleep wrapped in each other's arms until he wakes up again."

Chapter Eleven

William awoke three more times during the night. Once immediately after she and Thad had made love again, and then at four, and again at six. They continued to give him formula each time he woke up, though he wouldn't take much. And acetaminophen every four hours. He was still running warm to the touch at eight-thirty in the morning, when the three of them got up again, so Michelle held him across her lap, soothing him with gentle strokes, while Thad readied the thermometer.

"What is it?" she asked when he'd finished.

"A hundred and one point five, which is just above normal."

Michelle finished diapering William, then went to dispose of the diaper and wash her hands.

Because the tiny boy seemed content for the moment lying there on his back, she stretched out next to him on the bed. She took his little fist, kissed it gently. "I think his cheeks are less flushed, too."

William looked up at her with big eyes.

Thad joined them, stretching out on the other side of William. "He does look better," Thad decreed. "More interested in what's going on around him."

Thad reached over and got a rattle. He put it in front of William.

William's cherubic mouth dropped open in a soundless *O* of wonder. Reveling in the intimacy of the moment, Michelle smiled, too. "You think he'll run as much fever today as he did yesterday?"

"Typically, temperatures spike in late afternoon and into the evening, possibly through the night. He should be okay for a while this morning." Thad looked over at her, as relaxed as she had ever seen him. "Why don't you go for a run?"

It was Michelle's turn to mouth an *O* of surprise. He wanted her to leave? "Now? Are you serious?"

Thad shrugged. "You usually run every morning, and you didn't get to go yesterday. You've already told your office you won't be in for the next two days. It's a beautiful morning." He reached across William and covered her hand with his own. "Why not take a much-deserved break?" He smiled gently. "I'll stay here with William."

Michelle had to admit she was yearning to stretch her limbs. Running relaxed her the way nothing else could.

Still, she hesitated. "You really wouldn't mind?"

Thad brought her hand to his lips. "Parenting solo would be my pleasure."

The brisk breeze of the late-April morning caressed Michelle as she sprinted up and down the hilly streets of Summit. Flower blossoms were interspersed with the vibrant green of the grass and trees. The granite mountains rose majestically in the distance as the climbing sun lit up the cloudless, Texas-blue skies.

Spring was here, all right, Michelle thought dreamily. When she'd been younger, spring fever had hit her with tsunami force. Somewhere along the way, that force had dwindled, and the past couple of years, had finally gone altogether.

Now it was back again, fiercer than ever. And Michelle knew why.

It was because she'd found a town that felt like home. A child who made her realize just how much she wanted and needed to be a mother. And—most important of all—a man who respected her independence and treated her like an equal.

Life was good.

So good it scared her.

But, like Thad had said last night, they did not have to figure everything out at once.

They would put the adoption first and let everything after that slowly fall into place.

What counted right now was the joy she felt in her heart as she jogged up the street toward home, and the feeling of family waiting for her in her house.

Michelle slowed her pace as she hit the drive, walking the last thirty feet. She paused beneath the kitchen window to stretch her muscles. Hands splayed against the cement-board siding, she leaned in to stretch her Achilles tendon, and that was when she heard Thad's voice, coming through the partially open window.

"Thanks for the offer, but I'd rather not. Michelle?" Thad paused, sounding surprised. "Actually she's been of enormous help…. Yeah, she's still running as much as ever. She's out right now, as a matter of fact." Another pause. "You're right— that *is* one way to burn off excess energy…" Thad chuckled politely, as if hearing a quip he didn't particularly like. "Thanks, Violet. Like I said, I appreciate you going out of your way for me like this. Okay, catch you later."

Violet?

Michelle leaned against the side of the house, her heart pounding. More from what she'd overheard than from the exercise.

Why was Thad talking to Violet Hunter again?

Was that why he'd been so intent on sending her on a run this morning? Because he wanted to make a call he hadn't wanted her to know about while she wasn't around?

Fighting feelings of jealousy, Michelle strode in the back door. What she saw stunned her. Thad was standing at the stove, William strapped via canvas baby carrier to his chest. The little guy had fallen asleep again, silky lashes resting against his soft cheeks.

The junior cookbook she had loaned Thad was in the cookbook stand on the counter. The kitchen table was set for two. Thad looked so at home, so right.

This could be her life. And suddenly Michelle knew what she had to do. And the first order of business was not asking what Thad had going on with Violet. She spied the golden slices of bread sizzling on the griddle. "French toast?"

"It's actually not that hard to make," Thad said. Using the shaker she kept in the cupboard, he sprinkled some confectioner's sugar atop a stack of French toast that was ready to eat, added a pat of butter and a drizzle of maple syrup.

He winked. "I should've gotten one of these cookbooks a lot sooner. It's right at my level—beginner. Explains everything, including what a mixing bowl and measuring spoon is."

He sure wasn't a beginner in everything, Michelle thought, recalling the expert way he'd made love to her. Sensation sizzled through her, and with it, the desire not to screw things up unnecessarily.

Everything she knew about Thad thus far said he was an honorable man. She needed to trust that he was. Michelle smiled. "It looks wonderful." She appreciated the trouble he'd gone to. Glasses of milk sat on the table, along with a big bowl of strawberries. The aroma of fresh-brewed coffee filled the room. Surely he couldn't be up to anything significant with Violet. Then again, she'd never had a guy cheat on her. What would she know about infidelity?

And was it even that? Given the fact they'd never said they wouldn't see other people, not even when they'd been making love…

Oblivious to her tumultuous thoughts, Thad said, "Have a seat." He brought another plate over and sat down opposite her. "So how was the run?"

Michelle spread her napkin across her lap. "Nice." *Until I came home and heard you talking on the phone.* "Invigorating." To the point her heart was racing. And not from the exercise.

"Good."

She cut into her breakfast and found the toast tasted every bit as delicious as it looked.

"I need to talk to you about something," Thad said.

Michelle's mouth went dry. Pretending an ease she couldn't begin to feel, she looked at him and waited.

"As long as we're both petitioning to adopt William," he said, then paused to wrap a protective hand over the baby strapped to his chest, "do you think he should carry both of our last names?"

"I'M TRYING to be fair," Thad continued. He watched Michelle's cheeks go from pale to pink. Taking in her distracted expression, he said, "I like William as his first name. It suits him, don't you think?"

Michelle let out a breath. Whatever she'd been expecting him to say, Thad noted, that wasn't it. "Absolutely," she said.

"And Garner his last name." Thad hoped she agreed, because he felt strongly about that.

Looking even more relaxed, she took a long, ladylike sip of juice. "Right."

"But—" this was the tricky part "—we could make Anderson his middle name. That way, we'd be carrying on your family name, too."

Michelle swallowed the bite of food she was chewing. "I think it would be great to have him both an Anderson and a Garner."

"Then it's settled. We'll talk to Glenn tomorrow, ask him to amend the petition, or do whatever it is he needs to do."

Michelle nodded, obviously concurring.

"And there's something else," Thad said hesitantly. He hated to do this. But he had responsibilities he couldn't ignore, much as he wanted to today. "I was supposed to work eight to eight today. I got someone to take my shift this morning, but his daughter is in a performance at school this afternoon..."

Michelle didn't hesitate. "Of course you should go in to the hospital."

Still, Thad did not want her to feel abandoned. "I wouldn't go if I didn't think William would be fine."

"I know what to do for fever now," she reassured him.

Thad knew that was true. Still, he felt this odd, powerful reluctance to be away from them. Intellectually it didn't make sense. He knew William would get well without him. Emotionally, though... He knew what it was. That parental urge to hover. He'd witnessed other parents of sick kids doing just that when their offspring were admitted to the E.R.

It was time, he knew, to do what he had advised countless other needlessly worried moms and dads: go do what you have to do; your child's in good hands. Nevertheless, he couldn't help but add, wanting to be sure Michelle knew he was not deserting them the way his dad had often deserted him and his brother, "The hospital's only a five-minute drive away."

Michelle gave Thad the same look he'd given her when he'd encouraged her to go for a run. "What time are you going in?" she asked almost too casually.

"I need to be there by one."

"No problem." She began to eat her breakfast with single-minded concentration.

"You're sure you don't mind? You don't feel I'm running out on you?" Thad said. Something subtle had shifted between them and it wasn't to his favor, he was sure of it. Whatever it was had happened while she was out on her run. Had he been wrong in pushing her to go? he wondered. Had she somehow taken his consideration for her well-being the wrong way? Seen it as an invitation to put up the walls between them again? "Because if it seems too much to handle," he persisted, wishing they could go back to the mood they'd shared when they'd first awakened this morning and found William feeling much better... "I can make some more calls—"

She lifted her hand. "If I'm going to be William's mother, then I need to care for him when he's sick, too. And honestly? With him feeling the way he's been feeling, there is nowhere else I'd rather be."

Thad felt the same way. Unfortunately there was a shortage of E.R. doctors in the area. Getting someone in to cover a twelve-hour shift on very short notice was a real problem.

"We're going to be fine, really," Michelle insisted, practically pushing him out the door when the time came.

And that, Tad found, was that.

MICHELLE HEARD about the salmonella outbreak at the community volunteer picnic on the evening news. By 6:00 p.m., one-hundred-fifty people had been taken to the Summit hospital emergency room for treatment. More were expected, since nearly all of the three hundred or so guests had eaten the tainted potato salad.

Not surprisingly, Michelle did not hear from Thad until nearly eleven. "I'm on my way home," he said, sounding exhausted.

"Rough day?"

"And then some. How's William doing?" They hadn't talked since around four, when the first wave of sick people had started coming into the E.R.

"His temperature has been running a degree above normal, whenever the acetaminophen wears off. So I give him another dose and temp returns to normal. He just had a bottle and he's sleeping right now."

"You must be tired, too," Thad said gently.

She was. But it was a good kind of tired. The kind you felt after accomplishing something important. And nursing William through his first illness was extremely significant to her. The crisis, short-lived as it was, had let her know she was more than capable of being a good mother to this little guy. Michelle glanced fondly at the infant sleeping in the portable crib next to her. "I'm okay."

"I missed you today," Thad said huskily. She could hear the sound of his steps moving briskly across concrete, the engine starting on a nearby car.

"I missed you, too."

"Where are you right now?" he asked, his voice still husky.

She smiled. The come-on in his voice thrilled her. "Upstairs," she responded flirtatiously.

"In bed?" Thad persisted. The ding of a car door opening sounded in the background.

Michelle shivered, recalling the way they'd made love the night before. "Yes."

She could almost feel the heat of Thad's body over the phone. "I'm going to go home and shower and change clothes," he said in a low voice that sent her senses into overdrive. "Then I'll be right over."

Michelle snuggled more deeply into the covers. "See you soon, then."

They said goodbye and she hung up the phone.

The next thing she knew the phone was ringing. She looked around in confusion and picked up on the second ring. Thad's sexy voice rumbled in her ear. "You fell asleep, didn't you?"

Michelle looked at the clock, realizing only fifteen minutes had passed since they'd last spoken, but she had been dead asleep. "Afraid so." She yawned.

"Going to let me in?"

"I'll be right down." Michelle rose, padded barefoot down the stairs and opened the door.

Thad stepped inside. He'd shaved. His hair was still damp from the shower. He smelled of soap. And looked good enough in the gray jersey pants and white T-shirt to be in an ad for athletic clothing.

Upstairs, they heard a full-pitched wail.

Thad dropped his overnight duffel on the floor and, as they both ascended the stairs, said, "I'll get him. You go on back to bed."

Michelle wanted to protest. He'd worked all day, too, in the E.R. But one look at his besotted expression as he bent over the crib and hefted William in his arms made her realize that Thad had missed William, too. "I'll put him back to sleep," he said.

Michelle was too tired to argue. "Promise you'll wake me if he doesn't go right back down?" she said.

A now silent William cuddled against his broad chest,

Thad bent and brushed a kiss across her temple. "Promise." He hugged her with his free arm, then guided her down to the bed. "Now sleep."

The next thing Michelle knew, it was morning. Sunlight was streaming in through the open curtains. And her house was quiet and still as could be.

She hadn't set her alarm, figuring William would wake her at the crack of dawn. Instead, there was no baby sleeping in the crib beside her, no Thad in bed next to her.

Pulse picking up, she climbed out of bed and tiptoed downstairs.

Thad had opened up the sofa bed in her living room again. He was sound asleep on one side of the mattress, one arm folded behind his head. On the other side of the mattress, toward the center, was the Moses basket.

Michelle crept close enough to peek inside.

William was sleeping contently next to Thad. His cheeks weren't flushed. She touched his forehead—fever-free. Two near-empty baby bottles on the table beside the sofa indicated he'd eaten twice, three ounces each time. Which meant his appetite was coming back, too.

She was still debating whether to let Thad sleep or put the coffee on when the doorbell rang.

TAMARA KELLY stood on the other side of the portal. The social worker's swift, assessing glance took in Michelle's white cotton nightshirt, bare feet and sleep-rumpled hair. "Sorry to wake you. I thought, it being a Thursday, you'd be up, getting ready to leave for work."

It was after 8:00 a.m., Michelle noted.

"I was looking for Thad and William, and I thought you might…"

Realizing this was Thad's final surprise inspection before a formal report was presented to Judge Barnes, Michelle ushered Tamara in. "They're both here," she told Tamara quietly. "But William's been sick with a virus since Tuesday and they're sleeping, so—"

Too late. The doorbell and now whispers had been enough to rouse Thad. He sat up and blinked as if trying to make sense of the scene in front of him.

Recognizing Tamara, he lifted a hand in greeting.

"Mind if I have a look around?" Tamara asked Michelle.

Michelle gave her immediate consent. After all, she knew that since she was petitioning to adopt William now, too, she was subject to the same scrutiny as Thad. "The master bath and bedroom are upstairs, if you'd like to start there."

Clipboard in hand, Tamara toured Michelle's home. By the time she came back downstairs, Michelle had managed to slip into the guest bath and brush her teeth and run a comb through her hair. A sweater plucked from the drying rack in the laundry room and a pair of slippers from the basket next to the back door made her feel a little less exposed.

Maybe it was because he was a guy, or perhaps it was because he'd grown up without the same stifling set of expectations that she had, but Thad hadn't even bothered to comb his hair before he strode into the kitchen. Wordlessly, he gave Michelle's shoulders a quick, reassuring squeeze. As she smiled up at him, he smiled back and brushed another kiss across her temple.

Just that easily, some of the tension left her body.

"William still sleeping?" Michelle asked, realizing how wonderful it was to wake this morning and find Thad and William in the house with her, even if they had been downstairs.

Thad nodded and set about making some coffee with the

familiarity of someone who knew his way around her kitchen. A fact that did not go unnoticed by Tamara Kelly when she entered, making notes right and left.

"Can we offer you some coffee?" Thad said.

A buzzing sound rumbled through the house. It sounded like something was drilling through the wood floors. They all knew what it was. "Excuse me while I go get my pager," Thad said, "It's on vibrate."

Just that quickly a wail pierced the air.

Michelle rushed to go pick up William while Thad grabbed his pager.

As always, the infant stopped crying the moment she touched him.

Aware that Thad was now on the phone with the hospital, Michelle carried William back into the kitchen.

"He looks pretty good this morning," Tamara noted.

Michelle told the social worker what William's pediatrician had said, concluding, "This particular enterovirus only lasts forty-eight hours, so he should be absolutely fine by this afternoon."

Thad walked into the kitchen. "That was the E.R. I was supposed to be off today, but there's another wave of salmonella patients coming in. Seems everyone who didn't come to the E.R. yesterday for treatment is in there asking for care this morning. They want me to come in ASAP. So—" Thad looked at Tamara "—can we reschedule?"

"Certainly," Tamara said pleasantly.

Thad turned to Michelle. "I don't know what time you're planning to go into the office today—"

"Actually I'm not. I've arranged to work at home today and tomorrow."

"If either of you are worried about the impact on the department's evaluation if you have to go to work as scheduled," Tamara cut in, "don't. We have no problem with you carrying out your other responsibilities as long as adequate care is provided." She smiled. "William's sitter is a retired registered nurse with years of neonatal experience. She has no other children in her care. It would be perfectly fine for him to go to the sitter today."

"I'm his mother." The words rushed out before Michelle could stop herself. "At least I hope to be if the court accepts my petition." Her voice filled with emotion. "I think one of us should be with him until he's been completely clear of fever for twenty-four hours." Until they knew for certain that he was well again. "And since Thad has to go to the E.R. this morning, I think I should be here."

"I feel exactly the same way about our baby," he stated.

Our baby. Thad's words brought a thrill to Michelle's heart. His emotional admission did not go unnoticed.

Tamara wrote on her clipboard.

Thad's gaze settled on Michelle. "So you'll call me if there are any problems?" he asked softly.

Once again the world seemed to narrow to just the two of them. Michelle found herself in perfect harmony with Thad. Her heart warmed. "I promise," she said.

Chapter Twelve

Tamara agreed to stay and have a cup of coffee after Thad left for the hospital. Because it was also time for William's bottle, they adjourned to the living room to talk. Acutely aware of the sofa bed where Thad had been sleeping, Michelle gestured for Tamara to take a wing chair, while she pulled up the porch rocker that was now doing double-duty inside and settled into it.

For the first time in nearly two days, William latched on to the nipple hungrily. Michelle made sure William was comfortably situated in the crook of her arm, then looked over at Tamara as the social worker spoke. "I had an e-mail from Thad's attorney stating that you are joining Dr. Garner's petition to adopt."

"Yes."

"As William's mother?" Tamara prodded.

"Yes."

"But not Thad's wife."

Now came the hard part. The part Judge Barnes—and even Tamara Kelly—might not understand. "That's correct."

Tamara made another note on her clipboard. "What exactly is your relationship with Thad Garner?"

"Right now? I'd have to say co-parents."

Tamara wrote something else down. "Are you dating?"

No, but we are sleeping together.

Not trusting her voice to be even, Michelle shook her head. "If I had to characterize it," she said eventually, when it became clear Tamara expected her to reveal something about the specific nature of her relationship with Thad, "I'd say we are friends."

Tamara's glance slid to the sofa bed where Thad had been sleeping. It was clear she recalled the morning she had seen Michelle at Thad's house when the circumstances hadn't been so platonic in nature.

Tamara lifted one eyebrow in mute consideration. Finally she said, "Are you planning to date each other?"

"Dating" seemed a little redundant to Michelle, given the way she and Thad seemed to be so quickly and seamlessly blending their lives. "Probably not, under the circumstances," she returned.

"But you don't know for certain," Tamara pressed.

Noting that William had slowed down on his feeding, Michelle removed the bottle from his mouth and sat him up on her lap to burp. Holding his chest with one hand, she gently patted his back with the other.

"I don't think either Thad or I want to do anything that could undermine the sense of family we'd like to build."

"And dating would?" Tamara held her pen aloft.

"Dating could make things difficult later if it didn't work out." Although not impossible, Michelle amended silently, since she knew plenty of divorced couples who had overcome their romantic history for the sake of the kids. She looked Tamara straight in the eye. "Uppermost in our minds is what is best for William."

"I can see that." Tamara smiled as William let out a healthy burp.

Michelle smiled, too. "We both love him dearly." She situated the infant so he could resume his feeding.

The mood in the room turned overwhelmingly tender. "I can see that, too."

Contentment flowed through Michelle as she watched William latch on to the bottle again. She offered him her little finger, and he promptly wrapped his fist around it and held on tight. Michelle gazed into his sweet, baby-blue eyes while continuing her conversation with the social worker. "Thad and I want William to have everything he needs, and we both feel it's better he have a mother and a father even if the mother and the father aren't married to each other."

Tamara sat back. She took off her glasses and let them hang from the chain around her neck. Finally she said in slow, measured tones, "Judge Barnes always reads the social worker's report, but like the maverick he is, he doesn't always go with our department's recommendation. He prefers to make his own decisions, and as a judge, he has that right." Tamara's glance dropped to William, who had stopped sucking on the bottle and was staring up at Michelle adoringly.

Tamara continued with a sigh, "I won't lie to you. We have a dozen families waiting in the wings—families who've either already adopted, have been fostering or have been on waiting lists for a child for months. Families who know the story and are offering to give William a home, too. We're duty-bound to report that to Judge Barnes, too, since—under Texas law— he'll be making his decision based on what is in the best interests of the child, period."

"What's in the best interests of William," Michelle said firmly, upset at the mere suggestion they could conceivably lose physical custody of this little boy, "is for him to stay with me and Thad."

"I can see how much you and William and Thad have all bonded. I can see how much you and Thad love this baby." Tamara slid her glasses back on. "But I also need to understand how this is all going to work on a practical level."

MICHELLE HAD NEVER felt any sympathy for a woman who complained—after the fact—that a relationship wasn't working when she had never told the man in her life what she wanted.

Yet when Thad showed up at her door that evening, she found herself curbing her first impulse—which was to take him in her arms and give him a meaningful kiss. Instead, she ushered him inside and over to the Moses basket, where William was sleeping blissfully.

Together they gazed down at William. Tenderness welled inside her.

"What's his temp?" Thad asked quietly.

"Normal for the past five hours, even without acetaminophen."

Thad wrapped a companionable arm around Michelle's shoulders, showing her the kind of affection she'd always wanted.

"Looking at William now, you'd never know he'd been sick," Thad mused.

Michelle relaxed against Thad's body. "Amazing, isn't it?" she agreed. "How fast babies can get well."

"And sick," Thad said.

Michelle recalled how frightened she'd been when their little guy had first spiked a fever, how reassuring and strong and kind Thad had been. Not just to his son, but to her, as well.

He was an excellent father. A solid man and good friend. And a tender and passionate lover. Only one thing was missing in their equation. And unfortunately, according to Tamara

Kelly, that was the ingredient Judge Barnes was going to be looking for. She decided it was time to put herself out there, take a risk. She'd do it while they ate dinner. She looked at Thad. "Have you eaten?"

He shook his head.

"Me, neither. Want to order in some Chinese food?"

He grinned. "Sounds…just what the doctor ordered."

Thinking how easily she could get used to this kind of camaraderie, she made the call while he went home to shower and change. By the time he'd returned, the deliveryman was at the door. Assured William was still dozing peacefully, they took their order into the dining room. "Candles," Thad noticed, pleased.

And the good silver, china and crystal. Michelle took another leap of faith. "I thought we should celebrate," she said.

Thad's gaze locked with hers. "We do have a lot to be thankful for."

Indeed.

"So how did the rest of the visit with Tamara Kelly go this morning?" he asked as they munched on spring rolls.

Aware this was where it could get sticky, Michelle stirred sweetener into her tea. "She went ahead and conducted the formal interview for my home study."

Thad paused, chopsticks halfway to his mouth. "And?"

Wishing she didn't have to be the one to tell Thad, Michelle drew a bracing breath. "She had a lot of questions about our arrangement."

Thad leaned back in his chair and gave her a once-over that had her heart pounding. "I have a lot of questions about our arrangement."

A whole gamut of emotions radiated from her voice. "Me, too."

Suddenly Thad's mood became as cautious as hers. "Ladies first."

"Well." She forced herself to do what she did in every difficult legal situation—revert to the facts. Concentrate on what could be proved. "Okay, we're not in love with each other, but we do have a lot going for us."

Something flickered in Thad's eyes, then just as swiftly went away.

"Like?" he prompted, a hint of worry in his low, gravelly tone.

Michelle drew another bracing breath. Forced herself to look into Thad's eyes. "We're a great co-parenting team," she stated honestly, knowing that could not be disputed.

One corner of Thad's mouth lifted slightly. "Agreed."

Mentally Michelle went down the list she had made, since the social worker's visit. "William has bonded to us both— to the point that Tamara noticed and commented on it. So I know that will be in her report to Judge Barnes."

Thad looked pleased. "That's good."

"But—" finding she had lost her appetite, Michelle pushed the food around on her plate "—Tamara Kelly remains concerned about how this arrangement of ours is going to work on a practical, everyday level."

Thad's expression stated he had similar questions. "What did you tell her?"

Michelle shrugged. "The truth. That we intend to continue to live across the street from each other, even if it means I have to put an addition on my house. That we're friends. That we intend to be a family in every way that William needs."

"Without the wedding rings," Thad ascertained, a funny look on his face.

Michelle wondered if he was beginning to feel more than just a friends-with-benefits thing for her, too. But there was no clue on his handsome face. "Unfortunately that raised other questions for Tamara."

Thad's glance narrowed. "Such as?"

"She wanted to know if we were going to be dating other people, carrying on independent romantic relationships."

He went very still. "And you said…?"

Michelle tensed, too, despite her earlier decision to remain cool, calm and collected during this conversation. "That we'd have to get back to her on that."

Thad studied her in silence, his demeanor calm. He leaned toward her, searching her eyes. "Are we going to be dating other people?"

"I'll be honest." Michelle cleared her throat. "I would prefer we not. I know—" she held up a hand, as if taking a solemn oath "—it's selfish of me." She leaned toward Thad, too. "But our relationship with William is too new. We're still trying to figure things out and get in the groove. And to add another man or woman to that would be…"

"Messy," Thad concurred.

Michelle gulped. Inexplicably, joy began to bubble up inside her. "And difficult."

"Way too complicated," he added. His hand covered hers.

Sinking into the warmth of his gentle touch, Michelle had to force herself to go on. "I also know that you're a healthy adult—with needs—and I'm a healthy adult. And we're sexually compatible."

Thad grinned. He stroked the inside of her wrist with the pad of his thumb. "Very sexually compatible."

Achingly aware that all she wanted to do was make love with Thad—right here, right now—Michelle knew for both their sakes she had to stay on track.

So she continued with lawyerly calm, "Well, what I am

proposing is that we become sexually and romantically exclusive. We can tell the court that we're not seeing anyone else but each other, and that, as William's parents, we are in a committed relationship."

Thad nodded enthusiastically. Still, he countered, "You know what Judge Barnes is going to ask. He's going to ask us why we don't just get married."

Was it her imagination? Or did Thad want to know the answer to that, too?

"We'll tell him we're both a little too independent for that, that we like having our own space. So—as I told Tamara today—to avoid confusing William with that, we're planning to do the whole bird-nesting thing."

Thad appeared as if he had forgotten completely about that. "Right," he said after a moment.

Once again Michelle forced herself to push on. Just because she wasn't getting what she wanted—Thad, wildly in love with her and asking her to commit to him for all the right reasons—did not mean they could not be happy. Because the past few days they had demonstrated that they could.

Michelle withdrew her hand from Thad's and resumed eating her dinner. "Of course to really make that a viable option, we've got to finish the nursery at your house as soon as possible and start implementing our whole nesting process."

Thad resumed eating, too. "Anyone ever tell you that you sound like a lawyer?" He helped himself to more *moo goo gai pan.*

She added brown rice and lemon chicken to her plate. "I'm serious, Thad. We have to demonstrate that we can make this work on a practical, everyday level before we go back into court next Monday. So to that end, I'm taking off work tomorrow, as well."

"Well, you're in luck there, because I'm off, too."

"Now for the bad news." Michelle drew a breath. So much to do. So little time. "William and I went over to your house earlier today. And while the paint fumes are completely non-existent, the color is a little splotchy in places, which means the walls in William's room are going to need a second coat." She paused, hoping to enlist his cooperation. "I was thinking I could do it tonight—if you'll stay here with William."

IT WASN'T THE WAY Thad wanted to spend the evening. He also knew what was at stake. They needed to get this done in advance of the hearing with Judge Barnes on Monday. So she worked all evening finishing up the paint job, and then came home and collapsed in bed next to Thad, too exhausted to do anything but sleep. Early the next day she and Thad tackled everything else that had to be done. And while they were at it, Thad worked on a very special errand of his own.

"Hey, Thad," Hannah Callahan Daugherty, the proprietor of Callahan Mercantile & Feed, said when Thad entered the general store the next morning. She walked out from behind the coffee bar. "Violet Hunter said you'd be coming by."

Thad nodded, relieved everything was going according to plan. "I assume Violet filled you in?"

Hannah beamed. "She did indeed and your secret is safe with me. How's the little one I've been hearing so much about?"

"He's well and home with Michelle. How are Isabella and Daniel?"

"Great." Hannah beamed. "Adopting them was the best thing Joe and I ever did! But you're not here to listen to me go on about my deliriously happy family. Come on back to the storeroom. The item you ordered is in a box back there. You're going to love it." She pushed open the swinging double doors and led him to an oversize carton. "Both Violet and I adore ours. And speaking of Violet—you're aware she may have taken your request for help on this issue the wrong way, right?"

Thad knew Violet had gone all out to get the information to him. "What do you mean, the wrong way?"

Hannah shook her head in mute remonstration. "You men can be so dense sometimes! Violet still has a crush on you."

Thad frowned, irritated to be going over the same ground again. "We tried dating. It didn't work."

Hannah shook her head. "For you, it didn't. For her, well…"

Thad sighed. "So Violet thinks…"

"You asked her to help find this—" Hannah pointed to the box "—as a way of getting close to her once again."

Minutes later, still swearing silently over the misunderstanding, Thad loaded the bulky carton into the back of his SUV, then drove the short distance home. He was surprised to see Violet's car at the curb. He parked in the driveway, left his purchase where it was and rushed into his house.

Michelle was seated on the sofa, folding a load of freshly laundered hand-me-down baby clothes and blankets. Violet was sitting opposite her, still in her nursing uniform.

Their polite conversation stopped the minute he walked in.

Violet stood. "May I have a word with you?" she asked Thad.

Michelle looked upset. Not a good sign.

Figuring first things first, Thad turned back to Violet. "Sure," he said.

Violet murmured a polite goodbye to Michelle, then walked outside. By the time Violet had reached her car, tears were shimmering in her eyes. "Why didn't you tell me that Michelle was adopting William with you?" she demanded.

Thad hadn't made a secret of it. "I thought you knew."

"Well, I didn't. I thought—"

Thad cut Violet off before she could say anything else. "I consider you a friend. You know that."

"Right." She bit her lip.

"I want us to be friends," Thad continued. "I've always wanted that."

"Well, it's not what I want." Violet composed herself with effort. "I'm looking to get married again, Thad. I want my little girls to grow up with a father."

Thad didn't know what to say to that, except, "You're a terrific woman, an excellent nurse and a wonderful mother."

Tears rolled down her cheeks. "Just not the woman for you."

Thad's heart went out to Violet, but he refused to feel guilty. He had done nothing wrong. Instead, he gently reminded Violet of ground they had covered before. "Violet, we don't love each other. We never did."

"But you do love Michelle, don't you?" Violet guessed.

Thad didn't know what to say.

THE CIRCUMSPECT ATTORNEY in Michelle knew she should mind her own business. The emotionally involved, possibly two-timed woman in her had to go to the window and see what was going on out there.

Whatever it was, it wasn't good. Violet appeared to be both crying and ticked off as all get-out. Thad had that dumbfounded look men got on their faces when they were truly clueless about what was happening.

Finally Violet appeared to tell Thad what he could do with his good intentions and stomped around to the driver's side. Thad watched her drive off, then turned and headed up the walk.

Michelle rushed back to the clothes she'd been sorting.

Thad opened the door and walked in.

He looked over at the Moses basket, only noticing now that it was empty. "Where's William?"

For once Michelle was glad the little guy wasn't there with them. "Dotty called right after you left. She missed William and asked if she could see him. Once she was here and saw we were trying to get the nursery finished, she offered to take him back to her house for a few hours." She finished sorting the bibs and started on the onesies. "It was clear William was as glad to see Dotty as Dotty was to see him—she's the closest thing he has to a grandmother—so I said okay."

Thad folded his arms across his chest. He did not try to conceal his irritation. "What time are we supposed to pick him up?"

"Six-thirty," she said through her teeth.

He inhaled the delicious aroma permeating the entire downstairs. "Are you cooking dinner?"

It was supposed to have been a surprise for him. Now she was regretting it. "Coq au vin."

His eyes widened in interest. "That's one of your signature dishes."

She lifted one shoulder. "Used to be."

He came closer. "How long was Violet here?"

Michelle folded another onesie and set it on the stack. "Long enough," she said flatly.

Thad exhaled and ran a hand through his sandy-brown hair. "I'm sorry she had the wrong idea."

Michelle lifted her chin, angry all over again. "It's not surprising she did."

Thad's eyes narrowed. "What do you mean?"

"All those secret phone calls and messages that have been going on between the two of you!"

Shock reverberated through him. "If you thought there was something going on, why didn't you ask me about it?"

Michelle flushed. "Because it was none of my business."

He shot her a condescending look. "You preferred to jump to conclusions, instead."

She watched him just as steadily as he watched her. "It's no secret how she feels about you. Everyone in town knows!"

"Wait here." Thad walked out.

This time, Michelle did not go to the window to see what he was up to. She stayed on the sofa, folding clothes.

A couple of minutes later Thad opened the door again and hefted a big, bulky carton inside. It had a big red bow on it.

His mouth thinned as he brought it closer and dumped it at her feet. "I was going to give this to you tonight," he said. "But I think you need to see it now."

Michelle stared at the information printed on the side of the carton. "A jogging stroller!" she gasped.

Thad planted one hand on the top of the box. "It's your New Mom's gift," he explained patiently. "You know, what a husband typically gives his wife after the birth of their first baby. Usually it's jewelry, but I didn't know if that was appropriate in our case, and I've never seen you wear a whole lot of jewelry, anyway." He shrugged. "Then I figured you're a practical woman, so why not be practical and get you something you can really use? So I got you this jogging stroller. When you want to go for a run, you can take William with you."

"How does Violet fit into all this?" Michelle asked weakly.

He crossed his arms. "I asked Violet to help me because I knew she liked to run as much as you do and had tried out a few different brands of jogging strollers until she found one she really liked. So I called her to find out what the brand was, and she promised to get back to me right away with the information."

An array of emotions crossed Michelle's face as Thad finished telling all the details.

"But I couldn't write the product information down in front of you because that would have ruined the surprise," Thad continued slowly. "Instead, I waited until you were gone to call Violet again. Once I had the right model number, I ordered the stroller online and had it delivered to Hannah Callahan over at the mercantile, because I wanted to give it to you personally."

Never had Michelle made such a horrible mistake. "I am so sorry." She got to her feet and moved around the box to examine the picture on the label and peruse the long list of features. Then she touched the top of the box almost reverently. "This is such a wonderful gift, Thad, I hardly know what to say."

His gaze gentled in the way she loved so much. "I want you to have it," he told her gruffly. "You deserve it and so much more for everything you've done." He stopped her before she could interrupt. "And I'm sorry that my asking Violet for help gave her the wrong idea. Just to be clear—I set her straight a few moments ago, and I'm pretty sure she now hates my guts. Which is probably a good thing. She needs to find someone worthy of her, someone who will love her for the good woman she is. It's just not me."

Michelle knew that, too. "You were right to be honest with her, even if it hurt. As for the rest—" she released a pent-up breath "—I don't know whether to laugh or cry."

Thad wrapped his arms around her waist. "You were jealous," he said in satisfaction, looking down at her.

As much as Michelle wanted to deny that, she couldn't. "I don't want to think of you with another woman."

He hauled her close. "Well, that makes us even, because I don't want to think of you with another man."

"Then what *do* you want?" she whispered, thinking she already knew.

"You," Thad replied, "and only you."

Chapter Thirteen

Up to now Michelle had promised herself that she could make love to Thad without actually falling *in* love with him. She'd vowed she wouldn't let her feelings grow to the point she would be heartbroken if Thad didn't return her feelings.

But when his lips captured hers, she knew she'd been fooling herself.

She did love Thad, with all her heart and soul. It was apparent in the thrill coursing through her whenever he was near. The loneliness she felt whenever he was not. It was in the complete and peaceful way he made her feel at times like this. As if there was no problem, no difficulty, no complication they could not handle as long as they were together.

Rising on tiptoe, she wound her arms about his neck and returned his kiss. He tasted so good, all mint and man, and felt even better, the hardness of his chest and thighs pressing against her. She could also feel the hard evidence of his desire. She moaned softly as he clasped her to him and drew out the kiss until it was so wild and reckless it stole her breath.

He slid his hands down her arms, beneath the hem of her T-shirt, to lightly caress her back. His lips forged a tantalizing trail across her neck. Then he kissed her on the mouth again, deeply and irrevocably, until she thought she would melt from the inside out.

She moaned again, her need for him, surpassing everything else. The next thing she knew she was being shifted upward until her weight rested against his middle and her legs were wrapped about his waist.

Her pulse raced at the heat and intimacy of their contact. "Thad…"

He kissed his way down her neck, then back to the shell of her ear. "I want you, Michelle," he whispered, taking a sensual tour of her lips once again.

Desire shuddered through her. She felt her nipples beading beneath her bra, the strength of his forearm beneath her hips. "I want you, too."

His lips twisted mischievously. Then he headed for the stairs with her. "Hold that thought."

By the time they reached his bedroom, everything she felt—everything she'd once wanted to deny—she saw reflected in his eyes. He set her down next to the bed and held her face with both his hands. "Now where were we?" Slowly, deliberately, he lowered his mouth to hers.

His lips were hot and sensual, possessive and protective, tempting and erotic. She gave back as good as she got, running her hands across his shoulders, down his back.

"I think you were about ready to take my clothes off," she murmured, aware she'd never felt such power as a woman.

"And here I thought we were still at the kissing stage." He tilted her face up and kissed her again, and it was as masterly and dangerous and uninhibited as before.

Michelle reveled in the seductive demand of his mouth on hers, the erotic sweep of his tongue. She had never felt so wanted, so needed. The sudden unsteadiness of her body had her clinging to him, wanting more, more, more…

And he was just as hot and bothered as she was, his skin burning through his shirt, the proof of his desire almost scorching through the denim of his jeans. And still he kissed her, until Michelle thought she would drown in the tantalizing give and take of his lips. And only when she was pulsing with need did he shift his hands to the hem of her shirt and ease her T-shirt over her head. Her lacy bra followed.

The air between them reverberated with excitement as he took in the silky curves of her breasts and the jutting nipples. The world fell away and the last of her inhibitions fled. Wanting only to be his, she let him look his fill, let him bend her backward over his arm to kiss and caress the sensitive undersides of her breasts before settling on the sensitive tips. His caress was electric, filling her with erotic sensations unlike any she'd ever known. Pleasure flooded her in great, hot waves. Michelle swayed against him helplessly and let out a whimper she couldn't restrain.

Eyes filled with desire, he lowered her to the bed and took off her remaining clothes, except for her lacy red thong. "Beautiful," he murmured, and then that was coming off, too.

His lips drifted lower, past her navel, across her hip. Nothing had ever felt as right as the hot moistness of his mouth on her skin. Her eyes drifted shut as Thad parted her thighs and moved between them, creating ripples of need. She caught her breath as the sensations spread—until the aching need was almost more than she could bear. He held her right where he wanted her as her body arched. And then there was no more holding back. Passion swept through Michelle, her body now shuddering and coming apart.

And yet she still wanted more, wanted to explore the need pooled deep inside.

She shifted so that he was beneath her, then began the process of undressing him, too, uncovering hard muscle and satin skin. Taking her time, she showered him with sweet, sure kisses and slow, tender caresses. Until the fire flared out of control, and need had them shifting again, so he was lying on his back once more and she was astride him.

He reached into the nightstand and found the condom. She sheathed him, protecting them both. Then he cupped her bottom and lifted her toward him, his hands spreading her thighs farther.

Michelle opened herself up to Thad and he took her with a masculine ease that had her whimpering in pleasure. Everything about their joining felt wickedly wonderful and intensely sensual. Hands guiding her movements, he took her slowly, sweetly. Her heart soaring, she wrapped herself around him, taking him deeper and deeper. Their mouths meshed in powerful kisses.

And then there was no more holding back. The love she felt for him dissolved in wild, carnal pleasure. She cried out his name. Thad gasped out hers. They were lost. Free-falling into ecstasy that warmed her body and sated her soul.

"THAT WAS SPECTACULAR," Michelle murmured.

Thad rolled onto his back, taking her with him, holding her close. "More than spectacular," he agreed contentedly, sifting her hair through his fingers.

He also knew it hadn't been just about laying claim to the woman who wanted to be William's mother. Or finding some much-needed physical gratification for them both.

Making love had been a way to channel their feelings into the relationship without the burden of words. Or expectations.

If he had his way, of course, he'd already have them going down a much more conventional path—moving in together, instead of trying to figure out how to continue to keep one foot out the door while they got inevitably closer. He'd also have the legalities all wrapped up. The petition to adopt would already be granted. William would be his son officially. Michelle would be William's legal mother. And the three of them would be bonded together from this day on.

Unfortunately they were only days away from the next court hearing. Nevertheless, there was no doubt the three of them were a family.

And no doubt, from the way she was cuddled up to him with the aftershocks still coursing through her, that Michelle wanted to be with him every bit as much as he wanted to be with her.

The two of them were meant to be together, Thad thought, smiling at the realization that her legs were still wrapped snugly around one of his a good five minutes after they had climaxed.

They had time for one more bout of damn fine lovemaking, too, before he had to pick up William from the babysitter. Thad tumbled Michelle onto her back, slid between her thighs. "And speaking of spectacular…" He loved the rising excitement and passion in her eyes. He kissed his way down her throat, his body already hardening.

She arched against him as he made his way to the sweet ripeness of her breasts. "You can't be ready, Thad. We only—"

He took the tantalizingly aroused peak into his mouth. "Just watch me."

"BEING A FATHER agrees with you," Dotty noted when Thad arrived to pick up William an hour later.

"What makes you say that?" Thad held William while Dotty gathered up baby things and put them in the diaper bag.

"I've known you since you were a kid. I've never seen you looking so happy."

Thad *was* happy. And for more reasons than just the infant in his arms. For the first time in a very long time, he felt part of a family. Felt as if all things were possible. And if his instincts were correct, Michelle felt the same.

By the time he and William returned to his house, Michelle had set the dining-room table for dinner. Working like a well-rehearsed team, Thad gave William his bottle while she put the finishing touches on the coq au vin and tossed a salad. She lit the candles. He situated William in his infant seat, next to them. The meal seemed like a harbinger of many wonderful evening meals to come.

"I have to say," Thad praised as they dug into the expertly prepared chicken and mushrooms in wine sauce, "all those cooking lessons you took as a kid paid off."

Michelle grinned and handed him the basket of crusty French rolls. "You're not bad in the kitchen yourself."

She looked pretty in the candlelight. Content, just hanging out with them. Thad wanted to make love to her all over again. "I'll be better once I graduate from the junior-cookbook level," he promised.

Michelle chuckled and held up a hand. "You don't have to be good at everything, Thad."

"I want to be—for you."

Their eyes locked. Michelle looked as caught up in the raw sentiment of the moment as he was, and Thad knew life was good. Better, in fact, than he had ever dreamed. And when they took William upstairs to see his finished nursery for the very first time, his cup truly ran over.

Together, Thad noted, he and Michelle had done an incredible job of changing the former study into every little boy's dream nursery. A chenille rug covered the wood-plank floor. The linens in the mahogany crib were brightly colored. A matching border in the same car-and-truck motif separated the two tones of blue on the wall. A dresser that doubled as a changing table was fitted with a cozy, terry-cloth-covered pad. A rocker-glider sat in one corner. Cloth-lined wicker baskets held diapers and toiletries. A collection of toys and books filled the low bookshelf.

William looked around as they readied him for bed. When he was dressed and swaddled, they set him down in his crib.

"I think he likes it," Michelle said softly.

Thad wound up the music box on the colorful mobile attached to the crib rail. The sweet sounds of "Brahms' Lullaby" filled the room. Thad reached over and squeezed Michelle's hand. "He knows we're as lucky to have him as he is to have us."

By the time the music had stopped, William was fast asleep.

Michelle and Thad turned on the baby monitor, then went downstairs.

"Social services should definitely be impressed on their next unscheduled visit before the court date," Thad remarked.

Michelle's mood sobered. Thad knew she was likely thinking like a lawyer again and pondering all the things that could conceivably happen next. As a doctor, when waiting on the lab results that would allow him to diagnose and treat a patient, he often did the same thing.

He also knew that second-guessing what the experts were going to recommend was pointless. He and Michelle were already doing everything they possibly could—save one last thing—to make sure their joint petition to adopt William was approved.

Michelle frowned and stepped away from him. "Speaking of which…we need to talk about a few things," she stated.

Talking was the last thing Thad wanted to do. Especially when she was looking so on edge.

Knowing that what seemed unworkable at night after a long and tiring day often seemed quite manageable in the morning, Thad tried to buy time. Leaning against the counter, he studied the pink flush rising in her cheeks—the one that always appeared when she was on the brink of getting upset.

Telling himself there was no need to panic—Michelle was not trying to hold him at arm's length again but was just worried about the social services evaluation and Judge Barnes's decision—he asked gently, "Can it wait until morning?"

Words were not likely to help right now. Making love to her, holding her while she slept would.

Michelle shook her head. "Tamara could be here by then." She shoved a hand through her hair, pushing it away from her face. "We have to figure out our regular weekly schedule, figure out who's going to be taking William to the sitter when, and so on. Once we do that, we need to get the schedule typed up so we can give it to them."

"Can't we just make some general rules and take each day as it comes?"

Michelle's chin jutted out in the stubborn way he knew so well. "It's always better to have everything in writing," she said, sounding more lawyerly than ever. "And besides—" she gestured vaguely "—we need to figure out who is sleeping where tonight."

Thad had figured they would be sleeping together. He crossed the room to her side and wrapped his arms around her. "My bed is plenty big enough."

Her body stiff, she splayed her arms across his chest, wedging space between them. She looked up at him in frustration. "We're supposed to be doing this whole bird-nesting thing, remember?"

Thad regretted ever agreeing to such a ridiculous plan. Although at the time, it had made sense, he admitted reluctantly. "We made that decision days ago," he countered. "We weren't making love then, and regularly spending our nights together. Now we are." Now everything had changed…

She was becoming upset. "We only started doing that because William was sick."

Thad was beginning to see where this was going. He didn't like it. "It doesn't matter how or why we got close to each other, Michelle, just that we are." He didn't want to lose that.

"That's where you're wrong," she claimed.

"Tell me you're not comparing me to the situation with your ex-fiancé."

She was.

"I learned the hard way. It doesn't matter how wonderful it feels at the time." Michelle's eyes gleamed resentfully. "Traumatic bonding doesn't last."

"It could in our case," he said, "if we want it to, and I do." Knowing that the only way he could convince Michelle to see things his way was by being exceedingly practical, forthright and analytical, too, he gathered her in his arms. "I don't want to figure out which nights we're going to spend away from each other, Michelle. I want us to be more than a family of three. I want us to be a couple."

He paused, then decided what the hell—it was time to take yet another leap of faith. Time to convince her how truly committed he was to their future together. "I want us to get married," he blurted.

MARRIED! MICHELLE stared at Thad, feeling as if the floor had dropped out from under her. She couldn't deny she wanted to be with Thad all the time, too, but the thought of marrying him for practical reasons that had very little to do with the kind of romantic love she felt for him had her reeling.

She had been down this road before. Been with a man she loved, but who—in the end—did not sincerely love her back. She couldn't do it again. Couldn't risk her heart. Couldn't risk their entire future, because now William was involved, too. "I'm not playing around here, Thad. This is serious," Michelle said quietly.

"Damn right it is," he responded with genuine feeling. "Think about how much easier it would be. Think about all the benefits. We wouldn't have a disadvantage over all the other families who'd like to adopt William, too. There would be no misunderstandings—with Violet or anyone else—about what we mean to each other." His voice dropped a seductive notch as he continued persuasively, "No more women chasing me. No other men chasing you! No more awkward run-ins with the social worker. We could go to Judge Barnes next Monday as husband and wife and prove to him how committed we are— not just to William, but to each other and to our family."

Disappointment and disillusionment mingled inside her. "You've thought this all out, haven't you?" Michelle couldn't help it—she was beginning to feel a little used.

Thad's eyes darkened. "We have something special," he coaxed, linking his hands with hers. "An attraction that will last."

A physical attraction, maybe, Michelle conceded. As for love… Thad may have acted as if he loved her and made love to her as if he were crazy about her, but he hadn't ever actually come out and said he loved her.

Michelle had no doubt that if she were to make that a con- dition of marriage, he would dutifully utter whatever time- honored phrases she wanted. The only problem was, empty words and rote phrases weren't what she wanted, either. She wanted the kind of enduring love that had been lacking in her life thus far. She wanted a foundation of love for their family. Not just friendship. And certainly not just lust.

Because lust alone would not last. And when it faded, where would they be? Headed for divorce court?

The thought crushed her spirit.

She knew how hard divorce was on kids. She couldn't— wouldn't—put William through that.

So it was back to keeping one foot out the door.

"Listen to me, Thad." Injured pride brought a lump to her throat and she disengaged her hand from his. "Everyone who takes the plunge and gets married—for whatever reason— thinks they will make it. And believe me, as someone who practiced family law for five long years, I've heard every imaginable motivation for saying *I do*. But I'm here to tell you, only the couples with deep, abiding, real love have even a hope of making it for the long haul."

And the long haul was the only way she'd ever want a marriage.

"Michelle…" Thad began, reaching for her again.

She held her ground. "We can't do this for appearances, nor can we do it to enhance our chances of adopting William. Because if we go into that courtroom and what we say doesn't ring true, Judge Barnes will know it. Trust me, he'll be ticked off." She sighed. "And if that happens, I can almost guarantee you we won't have the outcome we want where William is concerned."

Thad grimaced in exasperation. Clearly he was very disappointed in her for not going along with his plan.

Unfortunately that changed nothing.

Moving away from him, she persisted doggedly, "We owe

it to William to stay off—not go down—a path that could potentially lead to heartbreak." Or, if they were very lucky, lifelong bliss. "We need to focus on what we know to be true—that we both love William with all our hearts. Everything else that has happened has been wonderful. But you and I don't need to *rush* into anything. Not when we can remain lovers and friends and co-parents and leave it at that. At least for a while. Till the initial excitement of adopting William passes and we can be sure our feelings for each other and the overwhelming passion we feel right now *won't* fade."

Thad looked at her as if she were a complete stranger. He clamped his arms in front of him. Stood, legs braced apart. "That's a very convincing argument," he countered in a low, silky smooth tone.

And one, Michelle thought too late, he'd heard before, to heartbreaking result.

"But I don't believe a word of it." Thad stepped closer. "This has nothing to do with what is practical and what is not. You're just afraid to love, afraid to believe in us and our future."

The ache inside Michelle intensified. She had no reply for that. Because Thad was right. She was afraid of putting it all on the line, the way she had before. She'd much rather hold on to what they had than risk wanting too much and losing everything in the process.

Thad shook his head in silent admonition. "You know what's ironic about this?" He threw up his hands and stepped away. "All along, I was worried that I was the one who couldn't make an intimate connection with someone. Well, guess what?" he said, his anger spilling over. "I was concerned about the wrong person!" He leveled a lecturing finger her way. "You've had one foot out the door this whole time, and you still do. You're the one who won't allow yourself to take the risk."

Michelle turned wounded eyes to his. "That's not true!" she cried, just as upset. She clenched her fists at her sides. "I'm committed to being a mother to William, and a companion and lover to you."

"Just not a wife." Bitterness tinged his voice.

She traded contentious glances with him. "We have to be practical," she repeated. "Marriage without love won't work. The rest of it will."

Thad's jaw hardened at the implacable note in her tone. His handsome features frozen in a blank mask, he countered with a willfulness of his own. "I'll co-adopt William with you, because I think he needs you as his mother, but as for the rest of it, I think we should go back to being just friends and co-parents. Nothing more."

The unexpectedness of his rejection was like a slap in the face. Wanting to be sure she understood what he was saying, she said numbly, "Not lovers."

Thad's muscles had turned to stone. "*Definitely* not lovers." He pushed the words through clenched teeth.

Tears stung her eyes. They had taken care to be so practical, to protect their hearts, their hopes, their future. How had it come to this? "That's really what you want?" she asked in a disbelieving voice, aware she had never felt more abandoned.

Thad turned away, a stranger to her, too. "It's the way it has to be."

Chapter Fourteen

"Thanks for coming in on such short notice," Glenn said the following morning.

Catching the veiled concern in the other man's eyes, Thad shook hands with his attorney and took a seat on the other side of the desk. "You said you wanted to talk to me about the adoption."

Glenn nodded and rocked back in his swivel chair. He rested his elbows on the arms of the chair and steepled his fingers in front of him. "I wanted to go over the specifics of the nesting arrangement."

Thad eyed Michelle's law partner warily. "Shouldn't Michelle be here for this?"

Glenn frowned. "I spoke to her earlier. She's already conveyed her thoughts on how it should go."

Or in other words, Thad thought sullenly, she did not want to see him.

Glenn opened the folder in front of him. "She would like each of you to parent three twenty-four-hour periods a week. And then every other week, you'll each have an extra day."

Trying not to think about the last time he'd kissed Michelle and held her in his arms, Thad shrugged. "Sounds fine."

"She'd like to care for William on the days you are working at the hospital. So if you will provide her with your work schedule via e-mail, she'll mark off her calendar, as well."

Struggling to contain his disappointment, Thad said, "Sounds…efficient." Which was just like Michelle. Only now she would be using that same preparedness to avoid him whenever possible.

"When she is in residence at your home, she would like to sleep downstairs on the sofa—and she requests you do the same at her home, when you are in residence," Glenn continued.

The thought of sleeping in Michelle's bed where they'd once made love and never would again was unbearable to Thad. It was understandable she wouldn't want any reminders of their failed romantic relationship, either. "No problem," he said tersely.

"She would like the nesting schedule to begin today. And since you had William last night and are at the hospital until eight this evening, she'd like to pick William up at Dotty Pederson's when she leaves work this afternoon."

Thad thought about the way William fixed his gaze on Michelle's face whenever she was near. "I'm sure he'll love that."

Glenn scrutinized Thad closely. "Are you okay?"

Thad did not know how to answer that. Yesterday at this time, he'd thought he had everything he had ever wanted. Now…if Judge Barnes approved their joint petition to adopt, he and Michelle would have a son to love, their homes and the satisfaction of their careers, but that was it. There would be no big romance. No sense of family, at least not the one they'd almost had within their grasp. And damn it all, he still didn't know why Michelle had broken it off. The truth was, he might never know. "I've had better days," Thad admitted finally.

"So has Michelle," Glenn confided. "I saw her this morning before she left for probate court. She looked like hell, too. Still gung-ho on being a mom, but otherwise…completely shut down."

Thad exhaled sharply. "I get the feeling you're trying to tell me something."

"I don't know what's been going on between the two of you except that lately she's been happier than I've ever seen her. And it wasn't just because she finally has a chance to become a mom. It was something more—and now that's gone." Glenn paused. "What did you do to make her feel so blue, Thad?"

"I HAVE TO BE honest," Tamara told Michelle during her last unscheduled home visit later that same day. "I didn't think this whole nesting arrangement was going to work."

Michelle moved around Thad's kitchen nearly as easily as she moved around her own. Doing her best to disguise her broken heart, she set a cup of hot coffee in front of the social worker and offered up an efficient smile. "But now you're a believer."

"Hard not to be!" Tamara broke apart a freshly baked scone. Beside her, William was seated in his bouncy chair, batting awkwardly at the arc-shaped toy bar in front of him.

"The baby is thriving. The nursery upstairs is beautifully done—he's obviously very comfortable there. Plus—" Tamara tapped the typewritten pages in front of her "—you and Thad have the scheduling thing down pat. I wish all our single moms and dads were as cooperative with their parenting partners as the two of you are."

Arranging the details of William's care via e-mail and text message was an easy task. Figuring out what she and Thad were going to say to each other when they finally came face-to-face with each other again was not. Thus far, she and Thad had managed to avoid an actual physical encounter by doing the exchanges at Dotty's house. But Michelle knew that wouldn't continue indefinitely. Sooner or later she and Thad would have to parent together...

Wary of the wellspring of emotion within her, Michelle sat across from Tamara and sipped her coffee.

She had come to terms with the fact that she would always love Thad.

What she couldn't accept was the fact that he didn't love her back. Because if he had, he would have given them the time they needed to make sure their feelings for each other were more than just a reaction to bringing William into their lives.

She swallowed. Forced herself to go on. "Thad and I both want what is best for William, no question. That's a powerful bond." So powerful, in fact, that Michelle had let herself forget all common sense and get swept up in a fantasy that couldn't possibly come true.

Tamara nodded, understanding. "I sensed that from the first," she said, then paused meaningfully. "I also thought the two of you might...well, have something more intense going on."

Michelle shrugged and felt her cheeks heat. She never had been able to hide her deepest feelings, which was part of the problem. Aware Tamara was still waiting for a reply, Michelle rationalized, "Adopting a child is pretty intense."

Tamara lifted a brow. "You know what I mean."

Silence fell.

Michelle ran her fingers around the rim of her cup.

"Would you mind a bit of advice?" Tamara asked eventually.

It couldn't hurt. Michelle swallowed around the growing lump in her throat. "Please," she croaked.

"If there is one thing I've learned in my years as a social worker, it's that every day, in every situation, we have an opportunity to construct one of two things—a bridge...or a wall." Tamara stood and patted Michelle's shoulder gently as she prepared to leave. "Make sure what you're constructing will get you where you want to be."

MICHELLE SPENT the rest of the weekend taking care of William, all the while thinking about what Tamara had said. By Monday morning she knew what she had to do. Risk her feelings once again and talk to Thad face-to-face.

Unfortunately he didn't come across the street until it was time to leave for the courthouse. He looked incredibly handsome in a starched blue shirt, dark suit and tie. His hair had been recently cut, and the tantalizing fragrance of his aftershave clung to his jaw. Michelle was inundated with so many memories, all of them good. Thad seemed equally pensive. And in some ways, unapproachable. As if he were ready for the adoption decision—and little else.

"Would you like to drive separately or together?" he asked, towering over her while she knelt to strap William in.

She thrilled at the low sound of his voice, the expectant look on his handsome face.

A bridge...or a wall.

The choice was simple.

Pretending to feel a lot more self-assured than she did, Michelle handed him the infant carrier holding William. "I think we should go together."

His eyes softened. "I do, too." Ever the gentleman, he escorted her down to the car, snapped the infant carrier into the base of the car seat.

"What do you think Judge Barnes is going to say?" Michelle asked nervously while Thad drove the short distance to the courthouse.

Thad took a deep, even breath. He kept his gaze straight ahead. "I know what I hope he'll say."

"Me, too." Michelle fell silent.

The next few minutes were consumed with finding a place to park, extricating William from his car seat, grabbing the diaper bag and heading inside.

Glenn York, Tamara Kelly and the court stenographer were inside.

They all sat down. The bailiff called the courtroom to order, and Judge Barnes strode in. As usual, the no-nonsense judge wasted no time getting down to business.

Tamara Kelly was up first. "I've read the reports," he told the social worker. "For the record—what is your recommendation regarding the minor child, and why?"

Tamara referred to her copious notes as she spoke, her clear voice laced with respect. "Although William is an infant and thus way too young to understand what blood ties are, there will most likely come a day when he is older when he will want to know his biological family, like so many other foster and adopted children do. Thad Garner can provide that essential link. In addition, it is clear that William has bonded emotionally with both Michelle Anderson and Thad Garner. They have worked well together to ensure that all of William's emotional and physical needs have been met." She looked the judge square in the eyes. "But what impressed me the *most* was the creative problem-solving used to address even the smallest concerns."

Tamara proceeded to describe their nesting setup in depth before continuing her assessment. "I have no doubt that Michelle Anderson and Thad Garner both love William very much and will make an excellent mother and father to him. Therefore, I am recommending to the court that their joint petition for adoption be approved."

Judge Barnes looked through the written report. He asked a few more questions. Stroked his chin thoughtfully. Finally he smiled over at William and said, in his usual gruff, irascible tone, "I was prepared not to like what I see here today, but it's clear this is one child who already has all the love and family he will ever need." Judge Barnes banged his gavel. "Motion for adoption is granted!"

MICHELLE WAS STILL a little teary-eyed and disbelieving as she and Thad left the courtroom, William in tow. Together, they accepted the congratulations of lawyer and social worker, then headed back to Thad's car.

"Big day," Thad remarked, his voice sounding a little rusty.

Michelle's throat ached with the effort to hold back happy sobs. She nodded, not trusting herself to speak.

"What do you say we forget about going home for a moment and take William for a stroller ride in the park instead?" Thad asked, his eyes as suspiciously moist as her own.

Michelle couldn't think of a better place to be on a beautiful spring day. And this time, she did find her voice. "I'd like that."

Thad got the brand-new jogging stroller out of the back of his car. Michelle helped settle William in the seat and strap him in, then the three of them crossed over to the green. The gardeners had been out, and the air was filled with the scent of fresh-cut grass and blooming flowers. Birds sang in the trees. Sunshine filtered through the trees. Children ran about on the playground in the distance. But on the path where they were standing, they were blissfully alone. William, lulled by the motion, was already asleep again.

Thad parked the stroller in the shade, then turned, took both of Michelle's hands in his and looked deep into her eyes. "I want us to celebrate today," he said, looking ready to make all her dreams come true and then some.

"I do, too."

"But first—" he raked her with a glance that was both tender and seductive "—I have a few things I want to say."

"Thad, I—"

He wrapped his arms around her and said in a rough voice laced with all the affection she had ever wanted, "I was wrong to try to rush you into marriage and walk out the way I did. You had every right to be cautious, given what you've been through."

"And you had every right," Michelle countered, with equal understanding, "to want more from me."

Thad tucked a strand of hair behind her ear. "The point is I should have backed off because I know that you deserve so much more than what I've given you so far. Not just time for us to get to know each other better and become a couple, as well as a family. But things like romance and flowers and candlelight dinners."

He wasn't the only one willing to sacrifice. Tears of happiness pricked her eyes. "Oh, Thad. I don't need any of that." *I just need you. And William and the three of us.*

With the pad of his thumb, he brushed away the tears trembling on her lower lashes. "Yes, you do," he insisted, the passion he felt for her gleaming in his eyes. "We both do." He pressed a kiss on her temple and then wrapped his arms about her waist, bringing her even closer. "I don't want to bypass this phase of our relationship. I want to savor every single minute of it."

Relief rushed through her. She laid her head on his shoulder and cuddled close, drinking in the warmth and strength of him. "I want that, too," she murmured.

He paused to kiss her, then threaded his hands through her hair. "Remember when I told you that I felt this immediate connection with William?"

Michelle nodded as hope rose within her. She splayed her hands across his chest. She could feel the thundering of his heart; it matched her own.

"What I didn't tell you," Thad continued, "was that I felt it with you, too, right from that first morning when we found William on the porch. And that scared me," he admitted. "Not because I was close to you, but because that felt better than anything else I've ever felt in my entire life. I was scared because I worried I wouldn't be able to figure out what you wanted and needed and I'd let you down. And what do you know?" he reflected bitterly. "I did."

It was her turn to confess. "Only because I wasn't honest with you," Michelle said gently, gazing into his eyes. "Because you were right, Thad," she conceded softly. "I was afraid to take a chance on us." The words rushed out before she could stop them. "Afraid that my loving you wouldn't be enough to hold a marriage together."

Thad paused. "You love me," he said after a moment, looking absolutely dumbfounded. And ridiculously pleased.

Michelle swallowed, knowing that now was the chance to lay it all on the line and hope that with honesty and time, they could make everything come out right. "Yes, I do. I love you with all my heart, Thad." The tears she'd been fighting spilled over her lashes and rolled down her cheeks.

Once again Thad was looking a little misty.

He flashed her a crooked grin. Eyes glistening with emotion, he bent to kiss her. "I love you, too," he professed, his possessive hold telling her every bit as much as his heartfelt words. "That's why I asked you to marry me. And that's why I want us to start over—" he paused to kiss her "—so this time we can take our time. And do it right."

Epilogue

One year later...

"It's a bold move," Thad said to Michelle as they toured a rambling Arts and Crafts home located three blocks from their existing residences.

While William relaxed in Thad's arms, Michelle and Thad looked around the second floor, with its half-dozen bedrooms and three full baths. All were in need of serious updating, as was most of the first floor. But structurally, the place was sound. It had two great porches, front and back. A yard big enough for a sandbox and a set of swings. And best of all, it had a study downstairs with a separate entrance, so she could work—and meet clients—at home.

Michelle squeezed Thad's hand, then leaned over to kiss William's cheek. "We're up to it," she promised.

Thad bussed the top of William's head, then her temple. He wrapped his arm around her shoulders. "Then let's do it." He grinned.

They proceeded to talk terms with the Realtor. By the time the sun set that evening, their bid on the new place was accepted. Their other two homes had For Sale signs out front.

The three of them had dinner together. Then she and Thad bathed William, read him stories and gave him his bedtime bottle. Minutes after he was tucked in, he was asleep.

They walked back downstairs, and Michelle stepped out onto the front porch.

A lot had happened since the previous spring. All of it good.

Thad lifted a brow. "Not much chance of us spending the night together tonight, I guess."

Michelle shook her head. He knew what tomorrow would bring. "This is one time-honored tradition we're keeping." She stood on tiptoe and brushed her lips across his cheek. "I'll see you in the morning," she promised.

BRIGHT AND EARLY the next day, she got up and put on her running clothes, just as she had one year before. At seven o'clock, the anniversary was upon them, and she went across the street.

As they had planned, Thad met her on the porch in the clothes he had been wearing the moment their lives became irrevocably intertwined.

William would no longer fit in the outfit he had been wearing that fateful morning, but he had on a similar white sleeper, with a blue sailboat embroidered on the front. "Dada! Mama!" William shrieked, waving his arms exuberantly as he played around the Moses basket he'd been left in. "Hi! Bye!"

Michelle and Thad chuckled. "Hi! Bye! William!" they echoed.

William grinned, happy his newfound powers of speech were being understood. Still babbling, nonsensically now, he lifted his arms high, letting them know he wanted to be picked up. And that, Michelle noted silently, wasn't all he could do. He had just started taking a few steps on his own. He was attempting to feed himself. Insatiably curious, he had the sunniest, sweetest disposition they had ever seen. "Our little guy really is thriving, isn't he?" Michelle murmured to Thad.

He wrapped his arm around her shoulders and pulled her close. "We all are," he whispered, pressing a kiss to her hair.

Having had his snuggle with Thad, William reached for Michelle. "Mama!"

Grinning, Thad handed their baby over to her.

Right on schedule, four cars pulled up and stopped at the curb.

William snuggled contentedly in Michelle's arms while Tamara Kelly, Dotty Pederson, Glenn York and Judge Barnes walked up the steps onto Thad's front porch. All had been part of the process that had welcomed William into their lives. All were clad in casual, Saturday-morning clothes.

Judge Barnes looked at Thad and Michelle and shook his head. "Young people are crazy these days," he complained in his usual crotchety tone, but there was an unmistakable twinkle in his eyes.

Michelle grinned. There had been a time when she was afraid of being more than co-parents to William, and family— in the loosest meaning of the word—to Thad. No more. The past year had shown them all just how strong love and commitment could make a family. Their baby boy had done more than just bring her and Thad together. Bringing up their son had shown her and Thad contentment unlike anything they had ever dreamed. And now, at long last, it was time for the next big step.

"Thanks for agreeing to marry us," Michelle told Judge Barnes. "Especially in such an unorthodox way."

"About time you two tied the knot!" the judge declared with a teasing smile.

"I couldn't agree more, so let's get started," Thad said, the promise of a life to be lived happily ever after in his eyes.

Her heart brimming with joy, Michelle handed William to Dotty.

She turned back to Thad.

Lovingly, he took her hands in his. They said their vows in clear, strong voices, and at long last, their journey as husband and wife began.

* * * * *

June 2009 is a month to celebrate in American Romance! In honor of Harlequin's Diamond Anniversary, we're offering four very special books by four special authors, including Cathy Gillen Thacker's MOMMY FOR HIRE, which features a bonus spinoff story from the wildly popular McCABES OF TEXAS miniseries!

*Celebrate 60 years of pure reading pleasure
with Harlequin®!*

*Step back in time and enjoy a sneak preview of an exciting
anthology from Harlequin® Historical with*
THE DIAMONDS OF WELBOURNE MANOR.

This compelling anthology features three stories about
the outrageous Fitzmanning sisters. Meet Annalise, who
is never at a loss for words… But that can change with
an unexpected encounter in the forest.

Available May 2009 from Harlequin® Historical.

"I'm the illegitimate daughter of notoriously scandalous parents, Mr. Milford. Candidates for my hand are unlikely to be lining up at the gates."

"Don't be so quick to discount your charms, my dear. Or the charm of your substantial dowry. Or even your brothers' influence. There are as many reasons to marry as there are marriages."

Annalise snorted. "Oh, yes. Perhaps I shall marry for dynastic reasons, or perhaps for property or influence. After all, a loveless, practical marriage worked out so well for my mother."

"Well, you've routed me on that one. I can think of no suitable rejoinder." Ned rose to his feet and extended his hand. "And since that is the case, let me be the first to wish you a long and happy spinsterhood."

Her mouth gaped open. And then she laughed.

And he froze.

This was the first time, Ned realized. The first time he'd seen her eyes light up and her mouth curl. The first time he'd witnessed her features melded together in glorious accord to produce exquisite beauty.

Unbelievable what a change came over her face. Unheard

of what effect her throaty, rasping laughter had on his body. It pounded a beat upon his ear, quickly taken up by his pulse. It echoed through him, finally residing in his stirring nether regions.

So easily she did it, awakened these sensations within him—without any apparent effort at all. And she had called him potentially dangerous? Clearly the intelligent thing for him to do would be to steer clear, to leave her to the tender ministrations of Lord Peter Blackthorne.

"You were right." She smiled up at him as she took his hand and climbed to her feet. "I do feel better."

Ah, well. When had he ever chosen the intelligent path?

He did not relinquish her hand. He used it to pull her in, close enough that he could feel the warmth of her. "At the risk of repeating Lord Peter's mistake and anticipating too much— may I ask if you'll be my partner in battledore tomorrow?"

Her smiled dimmed. Her breath came a little faster. His own had gone shallow, as if he'd just run a race—and lost. He ran his gaze over the appealing lift of her brow and the curious angle of her chin. His index finger twitched.

"I should like that," she said.

His finger trembled again and he lifted it, traced the pink and tender shell of her ear, the unique sweep of her jaw. Her pulse leaped beneath her skin, triggering his own. Slowly he tilted her chin up, waiting for her to object, to step back, to slap his hand away.

She did none of those eminently sensible things. Which left him free to do the entirely impractical thing.

Baby soft, the skin of her lips. Her whole body trembled when he touched her there.

He leaned in. Her eyes closed, even as she stood straight against him, strung as tight as a bow. He pressed his mouth to hers. It was a soft kiss, sweet and chaste. And yet he was hot and hard and as ready as he'd ever been in his life.

She drew back a little. Sighed. Their breath mingled a moment before she slowly backed away.

"Oh," she breathed. Her dark eyes were full of wonder and something that looked like fear. He took a step toward her, but she only shook her head. His outstretched hand fell to his side as she turned to disappear into the wood. This was the first time, Ned realized. The first time, since he'd come to the house party at Welbourne Manor, that he'd seen her eyes light up.

* * * * *

Follow Ned and Annalise's story in May 2009 in
THE DIAMONDS OF WELBOURNE MANOR.
Available May 2009 from Harlequin® Historical.

Available in the series romance section,
or in the historical romance section,
wherever books are sold.

We'll be spotlighting a different series
every month throughout 2009
to celebrate our 60th anniversary.

Look for Harlequin® Historical in May!

Celebrations begin with
a sumptuous Regency house party!

Join three scandalous sisters in

**THE DIAMONDS OF
WELBOURNE MANOR**

Glittering, scintillating, sensual fun
by Diane Gaston, Deb Marlowe
and Amanda McCabe.

60 years of Harlequin,
600 years of romance
in Harlequin Historical!

You're invited to join our Tell Harlequin Reader Panel!

By joining our new reader panel you will:

- Receive Harlequin® books—they are FREE and yours to keep with no obligation to purchase anything!
- Participate in fun online surveys
- Exchange opinions and ideas with women just like you
- Have a say in our new book ideas and help us publish the best in women's fiction

In addition, you will have a chance to win great prizes and receive special gifts!
See Web site for details. Some conditions apply.
Space is limited.

To join, visit us at
www.TellHarlequin.com.

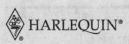

REQUEST YOUR FREE BOOKS!

2 FREE NOVELS PLUS 2
FREE GIFTS!

Love, Home & Happiness!

YES! Please send me 2 FREE Harlequin® American Romance® novels and my 2 FREE gifts (gifts are worth about $10). After receiving them, if I don't wish to receive any more books, I can return the shipping statement marked "cancel." If I don't cancel, I will receive 4 brand-new novels every month and be billed just $4.24 per book in the U.S. or $4.99 per book in Canada.* That's a savings of close to 15% off the cover price! It's quite a bargain! Shipping and handling is just 25¢ per book. I understand that accepting the 2 free books and gifts places me under no obligation to buy anything. I can always return a shipment and cancel at any time. Even if I never buy another book from Harlequin, the two free books and gifts are mine to keep forever.

154 HDN EEZK 354 HDN EEZV

Name	(PLEASE PRINT)	
Address		Apt. #
City	State/Prov.	Zip/Postal Code

Signature (if under 18, a parent or guardian must sign)

Mail to the **Harlequin Reader Service:**
IN U.S.A.: P.O. Box 1867, Buffalo, NY 14240-1867
IN CANADA: P.O. Box 609, Fort Erie, Ontario L2A 5X3

Not valid to current subscribers of Harlequin® American Romance® books.

Want to try two free books from another line?
Call 1-800-873-8635 or visit www.morefreebooks.com.

* Terms and prices subject to change without notice. Prices do not include applicable taxes. N.Y. residents add applicable sales tax. Canadian residents will be charged applicable provincial taxes and GST. Offer not valid in Quebec. This offer is limited to one order per household. All orders subject to approval. Credit or debit balances in a customer's account(s) may be offset by any other outstanding balance owed by or to the customer. Please allow 4 to 6 weeks for delivery. Offer available while quantities last.

Your Privacy: Harlequin is committed to protecting your privacy. Our Privacy Policy is available online at www.eHarlequin.com or upon request from the Reader Service. From time to time we make our lists of customers available to reputable third parties who may have a product or service of interest to you. If you would prefer we not share your name and address, please check here. ☐

HAR09